DEMON EMBER

M.J. Haag

Becca Vincenza

For Becca: What are we going to write next?
For M.J.: Everything.

ONE

I leaned back in my chair and rubbed my eyes.

"What is the point of math?" I asked. My roommate laughed behind me.

"The point is to separate the wheat from the chaff, Mya. The weak give up and drop out."

I spun in my chair to look at her. Our desks occupied a corner of our dorm room just outside the shared bathroom. Not the ideal location, but it freed up the space under our loft beds for a couch and TV.

"I think I proved myself by making it through the first year. I need a break. Do you mind if I turn on the TV?"

As roommates went, Kristin wasn't bad. Our personalities blended well since both of us were fairly mellow.

"Go ahead. I'll put in headphones."

I flopped down on the couch but hesitated to turn on the TV. I didn't think I had the brain power it would take to watch a show. I couldn't wait for winter break, still weeks away. Sure, I would need to deal with the stress of finals first, but it would be worth it to get away from campus. I loved going to OU Tulsa and living in the dorms in Walker. I just missed home and my family.

I picked up my phone and sent a snap to my younger brother. He was no doubt in the middle of a class. But as a senior in high school, he likely wasn't paying much attention, anyway.

This is my math-sucks face, I captioned the selfie.

A minute later my phone beeped. I opened an image of him trying to crawl inside a locker.

This is my escape plan, it read.

I grinned. Ryan was a goof, and I could always count on him to cheer me up.

Feeling a bit better, I stood.

"I'm going to grab something from the cafeteria. Want to come?"

Kristin pulled out one ear bud. "Nah, I'm good. Don't forget your pants."

I made a face. Kristin, like me, usually lounged in a shirt and underwear when in our room. The rooms were warm, and it was comfortable going pantless. Too bad the administration didn't agree. I put on my shorts so I didn't have to listen to another lecture about walking around without pants in public corridors, grabbed my ID, and left.

The halls were fairly quiet as I made my way to the exit. Most students were either in class or still sleeping. Given the option, I would have preferred to sleep in as well on my late start days. I wouldn't call myself a morning person. I just couldn't seem to sleep past eight. It probably had something to do with the fact that I had a hard time keeping my eyes open past midnight. I used the quiet morning time to get assignments done and relax before class.

I shivered slightly when I stepped outside and almost went back in for a hoodie, but I didn't have far to go.

At the Couch, our cafeteria, I helped myself to some eggs, ham, and country potatoes and sat at a table to eat. A morning news show played on the huge TV. They were talking about the protesters at the pipeline.

At the bottom of the screen was a news feed about increasing tremors outside of Rheydt, Germany.

"Crazy, huh?" the guy next to me said. "I was thinking of putting some money together to send some supplies to the protestors."

"I wouldn't. It's just perpetuating the need for the oil line. If the protestors really wanted to stop the pipeline, they would abandon their cars and their consumerism. If people stopped buying too much and using their cars daily or even weekly, we wouldn't need so much oil."

The guy gave me a disbelieving look. "Do you really think that's the solution?"

"No. I think less people is the real solution."

"What do you suggest? The Purge becomes a reality?"

"I'm not suggesting anything. I'm only pointing out that those protests are pointless. Most of the people traveled from distant places, using more fuel than normal to get there. The protest just puts more strain on the supply and demand system they are protesting. Sending them goods, like everyone wants to do, will only add to that demand."

He shook his head, picked up his empty tray, and walked away. I was used to that. I didn't think like other people did. My heart didn't automatically bleed for causes. I was too busy asking myself why a cause was needed in the first place.

Ignoring the protestors on the screen, I read the newsfeed about the earthquakes. The tremors began just after ten a.m. in Germany.

"Two hours ago," I said softly. The tremors started at a 2.1 magnitude that had increased to 3.9 already. Officials were saying the tremors occasionally occurred due to the Garzweiler mine, some miles south of the town. That was something I could relate to. Residences on the outskirts of Oklahoma City, where I grew up, often felt tremors because of fracking.

"You'd think we'd get smarter," I said to myself. I finished breakfast and made my way back to my room.

"Anything decent?" Kristin asked when I entered.

"Same as always," I said.

I took my laptop from my desk and settled on the couch so I could keep an eye on the news while finishing math. Kristin put her earbuds in, and we worked in silence for several minutes before she closed herself in our shared bathroom to get ready for class.

"Hold on, we're getting reports of unusual activity from our source in Germany."

The words caught my attention, and I looked up at the TV. The reporter was frowning and calling someone's name. A second later, a line crackled and the still image of a dark-haired man filled half the screen.

"Garan," the newswoman said. "Tell us what is happening."

"Another tremor just shook the area," the man said with a

heavy accent. "Some buildings sustained damage. The results are not confirmed, but we believe this one might be in the sixes. Local residents are being evacuated as a precautionary measure."

"What about the mining?" I asked the TV.

"Were there any injuries?" the reporter asked, instead.

"Minor injuries," Garan said. "The most unusual part of this last tremor is the animal reaction."

"What do you mean?" the news lady asked.

"Everything has gone quiet. I don't hear or see any birds, and the people I've interviewed in the last few moments noted that their pets have run off. One elderly woman said that behavior had decided her evacuation. To quote her, 'The whole place has an ominous feel.' I can't say Rheydt feels very welcoming at the moment."

"Thank you, Garan."

His line disconnected, and the anchor woman promised to keep the viewers up-to-date as news broke.

Kristin came out of the bathroom and opened her closet.

"Geez, it sounds like Germany is being hit by some wicked quakes," I said. "They're evacuating a town."

"Really? It must be a pretty big deal if they're reporting it here," Kristin said as she continued to get dressed.

"Yeah, they just had some news guy on from over there. He made it sound kinda creepy when he mentioned how all the animals have disappeared from the area."

As I spoke, the slightest vibration tickled the bottom of my feet.

"Did you feel that?" Kristin asked.

"Yep. Stupid fracking. You better hurry up," I said, glancing at our large wall clock. "And you might want a coat."

She quickly combed her hair before grabbing her things and rushing out. It wasn't long after that one of the girls from the adjoining dorm room closed our shared bathroom door, and I heard the water run again. We'd really lucked out. Our class schedules worked so we never had to fight for bathroom time in the morning.

I listened to the TV and worked on homework for another hour before I started to get ready for class. The talk of quakes and weird animal behavior had spooked me more than I realized because I jumped a little at the sight of my ghostly reflection in the steamed-up mirror. Shaking my head at myself, I pulled the hair tie from my long brown hair then locked both bathroom doors. Nothing about the news had been significantly disturbing. Yet, as I turned on the shower and stripped, I couldn't shake the disquieting feeling that clung to me. Probably too much stress and the need for a break.

As I washed, my thoughts drifted from the news to possibilities of going home for the weekend. Home was just over an hour away. I didn't have a car here, but Ryan would pick me up.

I turned off the water, dried, and went back to my room.

My phone beeped. It was an actual text from Ryan, not a snap.

Are you watching the news?

Just turned it off. Is it about the tremor that just went through?

I started to get dressed but only managed a bra and fresh

underwear when the phone beeped.

No, Germany. Turn on the TV.

Already saw. They've been having quakes for hours.

I finished dressing and read his next text.

A 9.0 just happened. They have it on in school.

Garan was back, but this time live, when I turned on the TV. The scene behind him was a pile of rubble and ruin. His skin was coated with dust, and the air was still thick with it.

"As you can see, this area was hit the hardest. There's still no estimate of how many residents hadn't evacuated in time. Rescue personnel are on their way." The faint sounds of sirens came through the speakers.

"Are you all right, Garan?" As the newswoman said that, something dark zipped across the scene behind him. The camera shifted slightly as if whatever it was had startled the camera man. A smattering of German broke out, silencing whatever response Garan had opened his mouth to say. Garan's gaze shifted from the camera lens to something just off camera.

"Garan?" the newswoman said.

"I'm sorry. It appears some of the pets are returning. Perhaps to look for their owners." The camera shifted to a pile of distant rubble where three dark shapes moved. "They appear to be digging," Garan said.

I stared at the screen, squinting to make out what they were seeing. With the dust still clouding the air, blocking out the already weak sun, it was hard to see the dark shapes they were talking about. The sirens grew louder, and the camera swept away from the rubble as Garan ran toward the vehicle to point to the pile of rubble. Since he switched to German, I wasn't sure what was being said. But the gesturing and concern on Garan's face had me thinking he was trying to get them to go check out where the dogs were searching.

A lone, deep yowl filled the air as the sirens suddenly silenced.

The news woman came back on the screen and again promised to keep the viewers up-to-date on what was happening.

The chilling scene of such devastation stunned me, and I yearned for home even more.

I'm thinking about skipping my next class, I sent to Ryan.

Life of a college kid, he sent back.

I shook my head, knowing I needed to go to class, and grabbed my things. The newswoman tried to contact Garan again but reported he wasn't answering. She speculated that everyone was working together to find survivors as quickly as possible. After expressing that the station's thoughts and prayers were with the community of Rheydt, the newswoman signed off.

I shut off the TV and hurried out the door. Campus was still quiet and chilly on my walk to class.

Arriving early, I took a seat toward the back of the room and set up my laptop, content to stalk social media until the professor arrived. Around me, the few students in the room were talking about parties that had happened the night before.

My phone beeped, and I hurried to turn off the sound before checking the most recent message from Ryan.

Go to YouTube and look up Nachbar von Hund angegriffen.

Is that German? I sent back before typing in exactly what he'd texted.

Yes. The video is just a few hours old and already going viral.

I made sure to turn off my speakers then pulled up the video. It started with a shot of a backyard from an upper window. After a moment, the back door of the neighboring building opened. A man stepped out with a gun. I watched him fire twice prior to something rushing at him and knocking him down. Before the camera could focus, the thing attacking the man darted away. I covered my mouth with my hand as the shaking camera stayed on the fallen man. Spots of crimson grew on his shirt and pants.

The man jerked, and I watched as he continued to spasm then stilled. The video had several seconds left to it. I was half tempted to turn on the volume to see if I was missing anything when the man slowly got to his feet. As soon as he did, he looked straight at the camera. The video stopped there, leaving me staring into his eyes. Something about them sent a shiver of fear through me.

Two

A door slammed shut, startling me. The professor continued to the front of the classroom, unaware of my near heart attack. I minimized my browser but kept my laptop out with every intention of taking notes. However, my mind returned to the video as the professor began her lecture.

I gave in to the urge to check social media after another text from Ryan. My feed was exploding with "prayers for Germany" and thoughts going out to them.

When class ended at noon, I started to pack up my bag. The ground trembled beneath my feet again. Not many of the students even paused on their way out of the room. Tremors in Oklahoma weren't a rare occurrence. I shouldered my bag and joined the flow out of the room.

My phone beeped almost immediately after the tremble stopped.

Did you feel that? Ryan sent.

Yeah. Stupid fracking, I sent back.

Tremors were near Irving, Texas. And we're feeling them here, he replied.

My stomach dipped as I continued my walk outside. We shouldn't have been feeling tremors all the way from Texas. The ones we felt here were usually from fracking to the north of us. Ryan had to be mistaken.

I hurried to my dorm building, eager to turn on the news to learn more when my phone chimed with another text from Ryan. I didn't look at it until I made it to the fourth floor landing.

Are you watching the news? This is insane!

I didn't stop to answer. I was in my room and had clicked the TV on a minute later. The channel was still on the news station from before. Streaming on the bottom bar was an urgent update: "There have been reports of tremors and earthquakes in Irving, Texas."

The door opened and Kristin came in with her bag strapped over her shoulder.

"Did you feel that?" she asked. "I was walking past Gould when I felt the tremor. My professor let us out early."

"Yeah, I was just leaving class when I felt it. The news is saying that it originated from Irving, Texas."

"Texas?"

"Oh, shit. Kristin, I'm sorry. I forgot."

"It's okay. Wichita Falls is about two hours outside of Irving. My parents should be fine." She sent a quick text off before she came to sit next to me on the couch. Only a minute later, her phone chirped. She looked at the screen.

"They're fine," she said. "No damage so it couldn't have been too bad."

We continued to watch the news for updates, but there wasn't much to report. Just a tremor that didn't destroy anything. Yet, I couldn't stop feeling a sliver of unease. First, Germany's tremors, and now, here in the States?

A very quiet rumble started in my stomach, a reminder that I hadn't eaten anything since breakfast.

"You ready to get something from Shades of Brown and some lunch?" I asked. It was a typical Tuesday run for us. She liked the Bolivian cocoa from Shades of Brown, and I loved the artisan sandwiches from Zoe's Kitchen.

She nodded and grabbed her keys. I took my wallet from my backpack and followed her out the door. We took the stairs to the ground floor level, passing other students coming and going.

"How about I drop you off at Shades of Brown and run to get the food? I need to keep working on my paper," she said.

I agreed, wanting to get back to keep my eye on the news. Little vibrations still rumbled under our feet.

It didn't take too long to get to Shades of Brown. Kristin pulled over to drop me off then left to go a few blocks down for our sandwiches. I walked under the black awning protecting the entrance and into the quaint shop. I inhaled the rich scent of fresh ground coffee and stepped up to the counter.

The tall barista with dark hair brushing over bright blue eyes smiled at me, starting a flutter in my stomach. I was a marshmallow for a gorgeous set of eyes.

"Hey, what can I get ya?" he asked.

"Two Bolivian cocoas please."

"Sure thing," he said with a wink and pushed off the counter to start my order.

I glanced around. I enjoyed coming here when I needed to get away from campus. The distressed wooden counters and small reading nooks made the place feel cozy and homey. There were always open tables, like now, to sit and take in the atmosphere.

"All right, two Bolivian cocoas to go," the Barista said, jarring me from my study.

I smiled and paid.

A tremor rolled under my feet, causing the hot chocolates to ripple. I held my breath as I waited for it to finish. I glanced up, and the Barista's brows were pinched and his lips were tight.

"It's getting really Jurassic Park out there."

He turned to me, his lips parting in a silent question. I forced a smile on my face and walked out. Not everyone got me. Fine, very few people got me.

My phone beeped, and I set the cups on the outdoor seating to check my messages.

Tell me you're seeing the pattern, too. #freaksbyblood

I grinned. Ryan was one of the few who got me.

Creepy coincidence? Anything on the news?

Kristin pulled up. I quickly got in, ready to head back to our dorm building.

Local no. Searching for anything new from Germany.

Once we got back to our room, Kristin and I immediately turned on the TV. We watched the local report, waiting to see if something would come up about the earthquakes in Texas.

Sent you a link, Ryan texted.

"Ryan tagged me in a new video from Germany," I said, moving to get my laptop before sitting back down next to Kristin.

I logged in and tapped the link for the video that had been live-streamed from Germany. Kristin muted the TV and watched with me as a man's face appeared on screen. He was breathing heavily and his eyes were wide. The image was dimly illuminated and bounced around as if the man was running. The angle of the recording changed as he lifted his phone high. I couldn't understand what he was saying and focused on the black he was recording.

For a moment, there was nothing but darkness and his harsh, gasping breaths. Then, I heard it. The clack and clatter of something moving in the void. Kristin and I both leaned forward. A growl started low and grew louder through the speakers.

"Is this live?" Kristin asked softly.

I looked at the time stamp. "No, but it was live."

The jerky aim of the camera caught a flash of movement in the darkness behind the running man. Suddenly, dozens of red dots flashed before the angle changed again.

My phone chimed, but I ignored it.

A blood-curdling scream made Kristin and me jump. We stared at the black screen and listened as the sound of growls and screaming increased. Something moved close enough to the camera light and was caught on video. It looked like a very large dog's leg. An instant later, it moved out of frame. Teeth flashed, and the recording went black.

Kristin and I remained silent. My sandwich felt like lead in my stomach. For a moment, I couldn't process anything beyond the fact that I was certain we'd just watched a man die. Then I picked up my phone.

Are you watching? Ryan had sent.

Why would you send me that? I'm going to dream of that shit now.

That's just one of the reports of animal attacks from Germany since the last tremor. It's like the wildlife freaked out and turned on us. Why aren't we seeing any of this on the news?

I didn't know how to answer Ryan so I turned the volume back up on the TV instead, to try to figure out what was going on.

"There have been reports of aftershocks in Irving, Texas. Viewers are urged to seek shelter."

Kristin jumped from the couch.

"I'm going to call my parents."

I nodded as she walked back into our bathroom. I texted Ryan.

Are you still feeling tremors there?

No. But are you still watching the news?

Yeah.

Did you see they announced communications are down in western Germany?

I hadn't heard that. Earthquakes...bizarre, aggressive animal behavior. I nibbled my bottom lip. What the hell was going on over there? And why was I feeling so creeped out about the tremors we felt here? I glanced over at our bathroom door and heard Kristin speaking to her mom. At least they were still safe.

Once Kristin finished talking, she rejoined me to watch the news. At 5 p.m., I got another text from Ryan.

Just heard from a friend in Wichita Falls. EAS ran a broadcast in Texas to stay indoors.

Without saying anything to Kristin, I changed the channel to see if we could get more local information.

"Due to reports of strange animal activity, people are encouraged to avoid animals showing any unusual traits or seeming unnaturally agitated. In other news…" The news anchor went over other safety precautions for Earthquakes.

"How's your mom holding up?" I asked Kristin.

"Good. They just had dinner. That last quake messed up the storage in the basement so they're cleaning that up."

If her parents weren't mentioning anything about the EAS, neither would I.

The station we were watching cut over to a program in progress. I tried a few other channels, but they similarly were no longer reporting on Europe or the tremors.

Kristin went to her desk and worked on her paper.

What's happening in Germany? Local cable sucks, I sent Ryan.

Reports of lost communication spreading. Friends no longer able to get messages to friends. Saw a message translated from someone in France reporting dog attacks in their neighborhood. Keep you posted.

I settled in to watch a movie. The room was getting warmer, as was usual in the evenings. Kristin opened the window a crack without me asking, and I kicked off my pants and got comfortable with a blanket.

It was around nine when Kristin climbed into her bunk, and I turned off the volume. It didn't do much good. Laughing and loud music faintly reached us. Somewhere nearby, someone was having a good time, and I heard Kristin move restlessly in her bed.

Near eleven, the music finally quieted. Kristin sighed, and I turned off the TV and climbed into my bunk. Someone called a goodbye in the hallway, and I closed my eyes.

All was quiet in our room when an eerie howl sounded from outside. Fear formed a cold ball in my stomach as I glanced over at Kristin, who stared at our partially open window.

The howl came again, sounding closer.

I grabbed my phone and scrambled down from the bunk to get to the window. Outside, the campus lights illuminated the view of the grounds, street, and distant parking lot.

Someone walked into view from the base of our building. He looked back toward the entrance and yelled goodnight just before another howl rent the air. The guy stopped and looked toward the south. Whatever he saw had him turning quickly.

"Get back inside," he shouted as he ran toward the building.

Behind him, in the distance, several shapes were moving fast. Dogs. Really, really big ones. Their thin, black bodies flew through the shadows, their eyes reflected red in the darkness.

"What the fuck is that?" Kristin asked.

The dogs were gaining on the guy fast. One sprang forward and knocked him to the ground. It closed its maw around the man's calf and shook its head viciously. I dialed 911 and lifted the phone to my ear. I listened to an all-circuits-are-busy message as the guy outside screamed and thrashed. Beside me, Kristin began to sob. More dogs converged on the man.

THREE

I started to shake and ended the call to try again. Screams echoed from outside and inside the building. Kristin and I weren't the only ones awake and seeing the attack.

Another guy ran from our building, yelling and waving his hands. The dogs stopped their violent assault, lifting their heads as one. In that moment, I saw they weren't really dogs. They had no ears that I could see, and their eyes glowed red. It wasn't a reflection but an actual glow.

"Get out of there. He's not moving," someone yelled from below.

Whoever said that was right. The man on the ground was a bloody mess. I couldn't be sure, but one of his legs looked broken or chewed off.

Behind the dogs, a car beeped and the lights flashed as someone tried using their key fob as a distraction. The dogs didn't even flinch. They remained focused on the new guy who had stopped waving his arms and was slowly backing away. He disappeared from our line of sight and the dogs howled, leaping forward.

The screaming started up again. Beneath those sounds, there was yelling. There were too many voices at once, but it sounded like there were people at the entrance, trying to hold the door closed.

Kristin turned from the window and opened our room door. She listened in the hall while I kept trying 911 and stared at the fallen man. What the fuck was going on? My mind played that panicked question on repeat until my fifth redial. That's when I saw I had a message.

It was from Ryan from about forty minutes earlier, thirty minutes before the music had turned off.

It's the dogs. Stay inside. Stay safe. Stay away from the infected.

I stared at the words, struggling to think and breathe. The dogs. Did that mean Mom, Dad, and Ryan had seen the same thing Kristin and I had just seen?

Are you safe? Did they come by you? I tried to send back. But the message kept failing. I tried to call and received the same "circuits are busy" message. I turned on the TV, and every damn channel had the damn EAS bars with a message warning everyone to stay indoors to avoid infection.

"Infection from what?" I said.

It took three tries to turn off the TV because my hands shook so badly. When it was off, I still heard the distant screaming and yelling.

"What's going on?" Kristin didn't have any better of an idea than I did, but I couldn't stop myself from asking.

She turned from the door, her face white. Shock. I'd seen it before when Ryan broke his arm. I walked over to her and tugged her back into our room before I closed and locked the door.

"You need to sit down." She vacantly stared straight

ahead as I led her to the couch.

"Kristin, you're in shock. We both are. But we need to get past it." Sitting beside her, I took one of her hands in mine and rubbed it aggressively. Doing something helped quell enough of the panic that I could think beyond "what the hell is going on?"

Those things outside were what we'd seen in the video. What was happening here had happened in Germany. Germany had lost communications, too. Why? What were those creatures?

"I don't know what to do," I said. "Ryan said the dogs are infected. The TV is saying to stay away from them."

She exhaled shakily and new tears trailed down her cheeks. I'd take crying over numb silence any day.

I stood up and went to the window to check on the man. I watched in horror as he struggled to pull himself in the direction of the building. Part of his leg dragged behind him, leaving a bloody trail. Chunks were missing from his side. My already racing heart kicked up a notch. He couldn't be alive. Not in that condition.

"Mya," Kristin sobbed. I didn't realize I was making noises until she spoke. I swallowed hard and turned away from the window.

"J-just freaking out. Did you hear what I said about the dogs?"

"Yeah. Infected. Stay away from 'em."

I took a deep breath and tried to calm the shaking. We couldn't both lose it.

"Right." I sat beside Kristin for a moment and rubbed her

hand again. "If the dogs are infected and they bite people, then the people they bite might be infected, too. We should stay away from everyone. Stay in our room."

She nodded, and I picked up my phone.

"Just stay here," I said to her before getting up and going back to the window. With my back to her, I slid the window open and got ready to take a picture of the man. He paused in his struggles and looked up, as if searching out the noises coming from our building. There were many. A lot of shouts and crying.

I snapped the picture and then zoomed in on the image to see his face. It was the same creepy, cloudy-eyed look as the man from the German video.

"Are they still out there?" Kristin asked. "The dogs?"

"Not that I can see. But there's a lot of yelling still."

There was a scuff of movement behind me, and I turned in time to see Kristin walk into our shared bathroom. She knocked on the adjoining door.

"Amy? Dawn? Can you guys open up?"

I hurried toward Kristin. "I don't think that's a good idea..."

The door swung open to reveal a very pale Dawn.

"Where's Amy?" Kristin said, looking into their room.

"Nate's dorm," Dawn answered. "I thought I was alone. Did you see outside? Why is he moving?"

"Who's moving?" Kristin asked.

"Never mind. Did you lock your door?" I asked Dawn.

"I don't know. I closed it when I heard the yelling."

I moved into Dawn's room to make sure her door was

locked. Once I verified it was, I used the peephole to look out into the hallway. Someone ran past. A door slammed shut further down the hall. The screaming and shouting was getting closer.

"Let's go to our room," I said.

Kristin nodded and led Dawn through the bathroom. I took a moment to push a desk in front of Dawn's door then retreated back the way I'd come. In the bathroom, I locked the door from the inside.

When I joined Kristin and Dawn, Kristin was looking out the window.

"Will you help me move a desk?" I asked her.

She didn't say anything about the man still dragging himself across the parking lot as we moved the desk. In the hallway, the noises grew quiet. I caught Kristin's glance at the peephole.

"Don't look," I said quietly as we eased the desk into place.

She nodded and moved to sit next to Dawn. I stayed near the door, staring at it. None of this seemed real.

A sound at the door made me jump. I held my breath, listening. The sound came again. A rasp of something against the other side of the panel. Swallowing and struggling to breathe quietly, I leaned forward to check the peephole.

A cloudy, once-blue eye stared back at me. I jerked backwards and covered my mouth. I would not scream. I would not panic. I would not die.

Our doorknob moved slightly. Not a turn. More of a jostle. None of us made a sound.

I waited, holding still and keeping quiet. Screams erupted nearby. The noise outside our door stopped.

I let out a shuttering breath that threatened to turn into hysteric sobs. No. *They'd* hear. I took a steadying breath and then another, working to control the hysteria. When I turned, Kristin and Dawn were staring at me with wide eyes. Their pale faces were a reflection of how I felt.

Outside, a smattering of distant pops broke out. Lifting a finger to my lips, I let them know to remain quiet and moved back toward the window. I couldn't see anything beyond the street lights. The roads were empty of traffic.

"I think we're on our own," I said softly.

I tried to move past the panic fogging my mind. What should we do? Should we stay and wait for help? It was smart. It was what people did when lost. Stay in one spot.

"We can stay here. We have water," I whispered, mostly to myself, "but only enough snack food for a day or two." It could work. Yet, I couldn't get the parallels between what had happened in Germany and here out of my mind. The video of the man being bitten then getting up. Seeing the man outside torn up and then dragging himself toward the building. And the cloudy eye in our peephole. The EAS used the term *infection*. Infections spread. Did staying in one spot make sense?

"Leaving means…" I turned to look at the door. The person who had been staring back at me wasn't healthy anymore. If we left our room, we would likely end up the same way.

I glanced at Kristin and Dawn and saw the same hopeless

defeat in their eyes.

More pops sounded from outside, pulling my attention back to the window. Nothing moved but the guy in front of the building. Even the screams inside had died down. I hoped it was because people were in their rooms hiding, not dead.

In the silence, I could hear the distant whine of several engines.

"Get dressed," I said. I pulled on my pants and yanked the sheets from our beds.

"What are you doing?" Dawn asked quietly, following me.

"There are people out there with guns and vehicles. We have two options. Through the door or the window. There's no way I'm going in that hallway."

Before we finished tying the sheets, Dawn pushed out the screen and waved her arms.

"I see them," she said.

We joined her at the window and exhaled in relief at the sight of several military vehicles followed by a line of cars and trucks.

"If you're not infected, come to your windows," a man yelled from below. His gaze swept up the building and over to the other wings.

He spoke softly to several uniformed men who broke off and moved around the building, out of sight.

"Stay in your rooms. We'll knock when it's clear."

On the far side of the vehicles, people emerged from the shadows, running in an awkward jerking way toward the sound of his voice. Before they got too close, the uniformed men standing in the backs of trucks, shot at them. The runners dropped with a shot to the head.

"It's real, isn't it?" Dawn said. "Zombies. Hellhounds. I'm not going to wake up, am I?"

I didn't say a thing. What could I say?

Instead, I stepped away from the window and helped Kristin move the desk from the door. I watched the halls through our peephole. Gunshots echoed from inside the building.

Several minutes later, a shot rang out on our floor. It wasn't long before a uniformed man knocked on our door.

"It's clear. You have ten seconds to open the door before—"

I opened the door not waiting to hear the rest.

"Stay close and stay behind me," he said.

We joined seven other girls. Behind us, two more military men guarded the hallway from where they'd come. An unmoving body lay on the floor. The hysteria I'd shoved down threatened to bubble back up. I turned away from the sight and followed the lead man.

We made slow progress through the rest of the wing, clearing other healthy people from their rooms, before we reached the stairwell. Our footsteps echoed as we ran down four flights to the ground floor.

Outside, another uniformed man waved us toward the vehicles where other students were hurrying to get into the back of the trucks. Through the chaos of evacuation, more infected ran from the dark. Shots didn't stop ringing. Dawn and Kristin pressed close to me as we waited for our turn.

As soon as everyone was in and the buildings cleared,

men with guns jumped onto the backs of the trucks, and the engines started again.

FOUR

"Where are we going?" I asked.

"The stadium for now. We're trying to establish communications to set up an evacuation."

When we arrived a few minutes later, we left the trucks. The uniformed men corralled our group from the university toward the stadium. As we jostled forward with the flow of the crowd, Kristin lifted up on her toes, searching for Dawn. Behind us, the vehicles pulled away.

"Come on, we'll find her inside," I said.

Together, we moved toward Oklahoma Memorial Stadium, our temporary shelter. We followed the herd of people to Gate 14, and the sound of our footsteps almost drowned out the distant shots and howls.

More military people with guns guarded the doors we entered. Inside the entrance, it was chaos, stifling hot and humid with the hysteric and shell-shocked people milling about. Some called out for friends, but most stumbled around looking lost.

Kristin tugged my hand, weaving us through the crush of bodies. The entry was filled with even more students and residents and so were the ramps and halls leading from it. People weren't spreading out or even thinking of the fact that the vehicles had left again, which meant there would be more people coming.

Kristin wedged through two people, pulling me. My sweaty hand started to slip.

"Hold on," I called out, but she kept going. I tugged her hand, stopping her. She looked back to me, her eyes wide and wild.

"We have to find Dawn," she said.

"Breathe. We're not going to find anyone in this mess. Look around."

Kristin took a deep breath and held it before she slowly released it. I did the same while struggling to think what we needed to do next. The frantic look in her eyes drained a little, and the stuttering of my heartbeat slowed.

"I'm okay," she said.

"Let's see if we can find someone who might be able to tell us what's going to happen next."

Kristin and I pushed toward some of the uniformed men inside the building.

"Can you tell us what's going on?" I asked the first one who made eye contact with me.

"Sorry, ma'am. At this point, all we know is that a State of Emergency was declared. Water bottles are being handed out at different concession stands. Our focus is rounding up civilians until we're told something else." He turned away from us to direct a family with a missing child.

Kristin and I moved back and roamed through the hallways, making our way to the rear of the stadium where it was a little less crowded. The gates we passed were either guarded by more military personnel or blockaded with benches and trash cans. The sight of all the men and women dressed in fatigues made it feel safe. Were Mom, Dad, and Ryan safe? I worried my bottom lip and followed Kristin, until the conversation of a group we passed caught my attention.

"Oklahoma City isn't that far. I say we drive there," a guy with a buzz cut said, piquing my interest. I tugged Kristin's hand and stopped walking.

"Who the hell knows what's out there, Josh," the only girl in their group said.

"Fuck this. We can't just sit around and wait," Josh said.

The two other men nodded, one of them pulling his shirt up to reveal the handle of a gun.

"We'll be fine," he said.

"Kevin," the girl said, yanking his shirt down. She fisted her hands and glared at each of them.

Kristin tried to pull me away.

"Hang on." If they were going to Oklahoma City—

A scream rent the air, breaking the tense silence between the friends. We all turned toward the source of the sound. A moment later, shots echoed further down the corridor. People started pushing our direction in their panic to get away from whatever was happening.

I glanced at the small group near us. The girl's eyes were wide. With grim, determined expressions, the trio of men moved toward the blockaded emergency exit.

I gripped Kristin's arms and forced her to look at me.

"Let's leave with those guys."

Kristin shook her head as the crowd began to swarm

toward us. Shouts rang out behind them.

"Run!"

"The infected broke through!"

"The army will take care of us," Kristin said.

"The infected have already gotten in."

"And they are shooting them. If you go out there, you'll die."

Further down the hall, more screams and shots echoed. The panicking mass of people rushed toward us. Staying here wasn't any safer than leaving.

"To the field," someone yelled.

I hugged Kristin quickly.

"Run, be safe," I said.

Kristin released me and took off down the hall, away from the mob. I ran over to the group of four trying to clear the exit. The third man struggled with moving one of the heavy trashcans. I helped drag it to the side while Josh and Kevin pulled the last remaining bench from the doorway. Josh pushed the door and it opened a quarter of the way, partially blocked by something from the outside.

"Stay close," Josh shouted before he ran out.

The screams grew deafening before Kevin then the girl hurriedly squeezed out. The third guy pushed me forward as the first wave of the crowd shoved to escape through the open doorway.

I ran after the others. Cool night air brushed my sweaty skin. My heart pounded. I knew what could be out in the dark. However, the waning moon was high, giving us enough light to navigate through the mostly deserted parking lot.

Josh and Kevin were already over halfway to the closest vehicle. The girl had fallen well behind. Panic and running shoes had me gaining on her until something moved to our right. When I looked, I saw nothing but shadows.

The girl ran hard toward Josh and Kevin, who were now at the closest truck to us. Out of the corner of my eye, a shadow blurred into something more, and it darted straight for the girl.

I called out a warning too late and skidded to a halt as a hound knocked her down. Its growls froze the blood in my veins. The hound's back arched as it bit down on her shoulder. My breath caught in my throat at her bloodcurdling scream.

One of the guys grabbed my arm and yanked me toward the truck. I couldn't take my eyes off the large, demon dog hunched over the girl. Her screams stopped by the time we reached the vehicle. Gasping breaths strangled my lungs. The guy shoved me into the backseat of the cab.

While Josh struggled to hotwire the truck, I looked out the windshield toward the building as other hounds ran into the mass of panicked people trying to escape. The hounds weren't the only thing chasing fleeing survivors. Infected people, ones who ran with an odd gait, attacked, too.

The engine finally roared to life, causing the hound, who'd killed the girl, to look up. Its red gaze locked with mine, and its lips peeled back to reveal bloodied teeth.

Military men came around the corner of the building and opened fire on the beasts and infected people. The first hound pivoted and snarled at its attackers. Blood flew with the impact of several bullets into its hide. Instead of fleeing, it charged toward the military men. They continued to shoot, and it kept running.

The truck reversed then jerked around before moving forward. We raced out of the warzone. People ran past. Some scared. Some with cloudy eyes. Then, it all fell behind us.

It's the dogs, Ryan had texted earlier. *Stay away from the infected.*

Was this really the damn zombie apocalypse? When I'd said we needed less people, I hadn't meant this.

"Breathe." The guy sitting next to me grabbed my hand and held it tightly.

I focused on each in and out breath, willing my shaking to stop. The driver swore softly as we sped through town. Once we were on the eerily vacant expressway, he glanced back at me.

"Who are you?"

"Mya."

"I'm Russ," the man gave my hand another squeeze. "That's Josh and Kevin."

"I'm sorry about your friend."

"Thanks," Kevin said.

No one spoke after that. Instead, we watched the roads.

Cars with shattered windshields were abandoned on the shoulders, and several of the infected staggered along the blacktop. When we sped past, they would run after us for a bit before they gave up. The fact that they kept up for even small bursts of time worried me, and I shivered as their dead gazes followed us down the road.

Once, out of the corner of my eye, I saw a flash of shadow

running on the side of the road, and I caught a glimpse of glowing eyes. Blood red. Like the girl's blood that had stained the beast's teeth. Another shiver ran down my spine.

The men were tense in their seats as we drove around more abandoned cars on the expressway.

"We are going to have to stop for gas," Josh said from the front. "It's almost empty."

Kevin spotted a gas station near the next exit, not quite halfway to Oklahoma City. Josh took the ramp and pulled into the empty parking lot. The lights flickered inside the building, but I saw no other movement.

"Kevin's got a piece, and I have mine. Mya? I'm guessing you don't have anything on you." Josh looked at me in the mirror again.

I shook my head. I hadn't planned on the apocalypse.

"Stay in the truck, then. Russ, you guard the back, I'll pump and watch my side. Kevin, you watch the front and the other side. Watch everything, Mya. Yell if you see anything."

In the silence after Josh cut the engine, we all waited, watching and listening to see if it was safe for the guys to climb out. Skeletal trees hugged the back of the building. Nothing moved but a few dead leaves in the wind. The whole place felt creepy.

It took a couple of minutes before Josh opened his door and the other two followed, getting out one by one. I rolled down the back passenger window an inch so I could hear them. Kevin's boots crunched on the loose gravel, interrupting the only other sound...the quiet hum of the overhead lights.

I watched Josh open the gas cap and remove the nozzle.

He swore and fumbled for his wallet. A beep echoed in the air when he prepaid, and the gas began to flow into the tank.

Russ moved to the end of the truck. I twisted in my seat and stared into the darkness surrounding the gas station. The shadows from the light of the building and the moon casted an eerie half-light. As I stared, the light seemed to bend around a certain spot. I leaned closer to the window and blinked, trying to see better. However, the spot had vanished.

Another gust of wind made the loose leaves on the ground rustle. The branches crackled together, and goosebumps prickled over my skin. I rubbed my arms. The fine hairs on the back of my neck rose.

The truck bounced ever so slightly, and I glanced out the windshield. Kevin stood not far away, staring into the dark. I looked at Josh and rubbed my hands over my jeans, trying to dry the clamminess.

Josh lifted his head. His expression went from impatient to worried as he focused on the back of the truck.

"Russ?" he called.

I turned in my seat again and stared at the back of the truck. The bed was empty.

I scooted over on the bench seat, close to where Josh stood.

"Where did he go?" I asked.

"I don't know." Josh's eyes were wild, and he kept glancing around as he continued to pump gas.

"Something ain't right," he said.

A bitter retort rose, but I swallowed it. Now wasn't the time to piss off the guy with the gun.

"Guys," Kevin said.

With his back to us, he stared out into the darkness near the road. I strained to see what he did, but saw nothing.

From the corner of my eye, something moved. I looked to the left and caught a dark blur rushing forward. I cried out. Kevin spun toward the incoming shadow.

One second he was standing, the next a blur of something lifted him in the air. I blinked at the sharp cracking sound, and squeaked when Kevin flew at the truck. He landed on the hood, making the truck rock. His neck lay twisted at an odd angle. My hand covered my mouth as I held in the scream lodged in my throat.

Something rattled against the truck. I glanced right, at Josh, as he frantically jerked the pump from the tank then moved toward the hood.

"Kevin?" Josh halted when he realized his friend was dead. He tugged his gun from the waistband of his jeans and held onto it with both hands as he looked around.

"What did that?" he asked.

I had no answer.

The light dimmed as something shattered outside. Glass hit the cab with soft pings. Josh looked at me through the window. A moment later, the remaining light went out.

There was a quiet sound behind the truck, like claws on blacktop. I jumped and twisted around in my seat thinking of the man outside of my dorm room. He'd been the first to die, then the guy's friend. It was happening again, and I would be next. My breaths came in heavy pants, and I frantically searched the darkness, struggling to find the thing that would kill me.

Something moved just in front of the truck. I caught a glimpse of grey skin and thick limbs.

Josh pulled the trigger, and the noise made me flinch. The shadow kept moving. Josh shot again.

Bam.

Bam.

Bam.

Click.

The shadow leapt into the air toward the truck, and Josh let out a shocked grunt-scream.

The metal above me bent inward as the creature landed on top of the cab. I squealed and crouched lower in my seat, unable to take my eyes from Josh. His eyes rounded as he stared up at whatever had landed on the roof of the truck. I could barely breathe past the fear squeezing my chest.

I jolted when something jumped from the top and landed in front of Josh. It rose from a partial crouch to its full height. A man. Impossibly huge. His biceps were as big as my head, but...he wasn't human. His grey skin, and pointed ears that poked out from the long black hair he had pulled into a twisted ponytail hanging down his back, made him very not human.

Josh's face paled further.

"Wh-what...?" he breathed.

The thing reached out, gripped Josh's neck with one hand, and twisted. Josh's face went slack, and the thing released its hold. Josh fell limply out of sight.

I looked at Kevin, who lay draped over the hood, then frantically scrambled across the seat, getting as far away as I could from the thing that had killed everyone else.

It heard me and slowly turned around.

FIVE

Green eyes with reptilian pupils stared at me through the window.

I couldn't breathe. My heart thundered in my ears. I was going to die. I thought of my family and hoped they wouldn't suffer the same fate.

The creature leaned toward the glass. His gaze shifted from my head to my body then back up again. Though I shook uncontrollably, I couldn't look away from his eyes. The black vertical slit of his pupils interrupted the otherwise solid bright green of the rest of his eyes.

Finally, he pulled back from the window to study the glass separating us. Specifically, the one inch gap at the top.

Shit. The leather squeaked under me as I shifted in my seat.

His gaze snapped to mine again. His complete stillness motivated me. He was the hunter. I was the prey. I needed to get my ass moving. Sitting there waiting to die wasn't an option.

I glanced over the front seat at the wires hanging below the dash. A simple connection. I could do it. Start the truck and drive off before that thing figured out the flimsy piece of glass separating us posed no problem.

When I looked back at the window, the creature had vanished. I didn't hesitate. I climbed over the seat and grabbed for the wires. A shock zapped through me, and I yelped. But I didn't stop trying. The engine turned over once then started.

Something thumped on the hood, making the truck bounce slightly. I flinched and looked up, expecting to see the creature. Instead, Kevin's body slowly slid away from the windshield and over the edge. For a horror-filled moment, I could only think about how I would need to drive over him to get away.

Movement next to my window made me jump, and I turned my head. Yellow-green eyes met mine. I froze, afraid to move. My heart felt like it wanted to pound its way out of my chest. He watched me as I watched him. His focus made me very aware that I needed to do something soon. My shaking was only getting worse. If I continued to hesitate, I'd end up dead like the rest.

My knees still pressed against the seat, my feet nowhere near the pedals. I grabbed the wheel and started to swing my legs to the side. He slammed his open hand against the window. The glass splintered and folded in toward me. He reached in, his hand wrapped around my left arm.

I yelped and pulled back, no longer caring about lunging for the pedals. He reached in with his other hand, grabbed me under the right armpit, and dragged me forward. The steering wheel slipped from my grasp. I tried for it once more but missed as he yanked my upper body out the window. I reared back, flailing. His hold under my right arm slipped, and I struggled to pull myself back in. He reached for me again, missed my arm, and grabbed my boob.

He jerked his hand back, and I froze, staring at him with wide-eyes as I hung out the window, pinned in place by his other hand. He reached forward with his free hand, and I put my arm up, trying to protect my neck.

His palm covered my right boob, and he gave it another tentative squeeze. I lowered my arm in shock and watched him pull back once more. His gaze zeroed in on my left side.

"Hell no," I said, renewing my struggles.

As if his first attempt to remove me had just been a test, he plucked me out of the truck and set me on my feet in front of him. He kept his right hand firmly anchored around my upper arm as he lifted his other hand.

My chest heaved with each panicked breath. When his hand got close to my boob, I swatted it away.

He grunted, lowered his hand to his side, and studied me. When his gaze dropped to my jeans, a new panic surged forth. I pulled hard, willing to yank off my own arm to get away from him. He backed me against the truck, limiting my struggles, and proceeded to pat down the front of my jeans.

"No...no...just kill me already."

He stopped patting and sniffed my hair, my ears, and my face. Shock kept me still for most of it.

Abruptly, he let go and stepped back. We stared at each other as my pulse thundered in my ears. What the hell was going on? Was he toying with me?

The truck still rumbled behind me, a possible means of escape if I could just get inside. With the door handle digging into my back, I edged to the left. He put his hand on the door, stopping my progress. I bolted the other direction. He moved incredibly fast, blocking me by the front tire.

With a growl, he turned toward the hood. He raised his fisted hands and brought them down on the hood. I jumped at the sound of metal crunching on impact. He hit the front of the truck again and again, crushing the metal in until the engine clunked several times then died.

I took an involuntary step back. He'd just smashed a truck with his bare hands. I swallowed hard, and it took a moment to realize he'd killed any means of escape. I stared at him, out of ideas and out of hope.

He wasn't even breathing heavily, just standing there watching me. When he saw he had my attention, he reached up and pulled the cord holding his shirt together at his throat. Within seconds, he had the loose-fitting dark shirt off.

I stared at his heavily muscled torso with increasing despair.

He tilted his head at me, then reached up and patted his chest. First one side, then the other. When he reached for me, I cringed back. It didn't deter him. He followed me and patted first one boob then the other before tugging at my long-sleeved shirt.

My brain struggled to process what was happening.

"I don't want to take off my clothes."

He tilted his head again and waited for a moment. When he reached for the cord at the waist of his pants, I squeaked. My reaction didn't stop him from shoving the dark material down far enough to show me his grey package with a penis longer than any human version I'd ever seen. Not that I'd seen many in person.

He palmed himself as if saying "see, this is what I'm offering you" and watched me expectantly.

"No, thank you."

He shook himself again and, in that moment, I understood he was attempting to communicate.

"I-I don't want to play Tarzan and Jane."

He tilted his head at me again, as if listening to my words.

"Let me go. Please, just let me go."

He slowly pulled the material up around his hips and tied it. When he picked up his shirt, I got ready. Glass crunched under my shoe as I shifted my weight to my right foot. He stopped putting on his shirt and tucked it into the waist of his pants, instead.

Scratching his ear lightly, he continued to watch me like I was some kind of puzzle. I didn't want to be figured out. I wanted to be let go. Like right now.

He looked at my crotch, my boobs, and my hair once more then grabbed his shirt. As soon as he had his head covered, I took off. I only made it a step before he caught me from behind and lifted me off my feet. With one arm wrapped around my waist, he groped me with the other. This time between my legs.

I twisted and kicked, trying to get free. He didn't even seem to notice.

Suddenly, I stood on my own two feet again. I spun around to face him, backing away a step. However, I no longer had his attention. Cringing, I watched him lift his hand to his nose. He sniffed.

A sound of disbelief escaped me, and he met my gaze. If he would have licked his fingers, I would have known he saw me as a walking meat stick. Instead, he slowly lowered his hand.

"What is going on?" I said in a half whisper, half whimper. Did he plan to kill me or not? My chest felt so tight I was pretty sure my stuttering heart would give out any minute. Death by fear or death by…whatever he was. The method didn't change the end result. Death.

Swallowing hard, I closed my eyes and resigned myself to that fact. If I was going to die, I would rather die trying to get away. I opened my eyes, turned, and started walking. Nothing happened. Well, not nothing. Gravel crunched behind me. I glanced back to see him studying my walk as he followed me. I didn't try to guess what that might signify; I just kept going.

At the edge of the road, I hesitated. Infected riddled the not too distant highway, making the easiest route, the most dangerous. That meant hiking through the fields and trees. I crossed the road and started through the field, angling slightly away from the highway.

The crunch of dry grass under my shoes made me cringe. Behind me, a softer footfall echoed each of my own.

Although I felt beyond confused and scared, a sort of numbness had slowly crept in, blanketing me from my current reality. A reality where black, dog-like creatures with red eyes were running around biting people and turning normal humans into things resembling zombies. And, as if that hadn't been a hard enough reality to grip, a man with grey skin, pointy ears, and slitted eyes had just killed the three guys with me. I couldn't even think about the groping that had also taken place.

What the hell was going on? How had life gotten so messed up? For a brief moment, I thought of Kristin and wondered if my fate would have been any better if I'd stayed with her at the stadium. I should have been sleeping now, not trying to figure out how to get to Oklahoma City while avoiding zombie infested roadways.

Suddenly, the creature stood in front of me. I barely stopped in time to avoid colliding with his chest.

"What do you want from me?" I asked, my voice shaking. I was ready to crash hard, mentally and physically. And, I desperately needed my version of reality back.

He opened his mouth and spoke, or at least made sounds, but I didn't hear much. My attention locked onto his very pointed canines. It took me a moment to realize he'd stopped making sounds.

Barely breathing, I took a slow step back from him. He shadowed me, stepping into my retreat. I moved faster. He stalked me. I stopped. He stopped. We stared at each other.

Holding my gaze, he started to lean in.

"Go away," I said softly.

He didn't stop his approach.

"If you try grabbing me again, I'm aiming for your balls." I remembered Kevin's broken neck and the way his body had draped the hood and regretted my words.

When the creature started to bend his knees, my stomach gave a sickening lurch. I moved to step back, and he grabbed both my arms. Instead of breaking my neck or throwing me, he held me in place as he buried his nose in my shirt-covered cleavage. Since I had a decent amount, he had to wiggle a little to really get his face in there. He inhaled deeply, then pulled back to look at me.

Scared shitless but pretending not to be, I glared at him.

"Get a good smell?" Instead of indignant and angry, my voice shook pathetically.

He blinked at me again, and I wondered why I still lived. Despite his groping and weird sniffing, he hadn't been aroused when he'd pulled down his pants. Thank God. However, that left me completely clueless regarding the current staring contest.

SIX

In the dim moonlight, I tried to see past his large, eerie eyes and focus on his other features, like his thick black eyebrows and his very strong, stubborn jaw. His pointed ears were longer than normal. Well, longer than a normal human's ears, by about two inches.

He let go of my left arm, reached up to touch the tip of the ear I was studying, then reached out to brush back my hair. It took all my will not to jerk away. His fingers brushed the outer shell of my ear, then he leaned in for a closer look.

He seemed curious. But that didn't make sense. If he was this curious about humans, why did he kill everyone else?

"It's an ear," I said, finally.

His gaze met mine, and he gently touched my ear again.

Hoping that he was curious and not just deciding how to kill me, I reached up and carefully grabbed the wrist of the hand clamped around my right arm. His hold immediately loosened, and he straightened away from me.

Free, I sidestepped him and started walking again. Each footfall thumped in time with my racing heart. While I almost jogged, the creature beside me kept up with long, loose strides. We made it several yards before he stepped in front of me again.

My sanity cracked.

"No," I said, bringing up a finger to scold him as if he were a bad dog. "If you don't quit stopping me, one of those hellhounds is going to find us. We're too close to the highway. I need to keep moving or I'll never make it home."

I couldn't believe what I'd done. Swallowing past the lump of terror in my throat, I went around him once more. He didn't try to block me or get handsy again. But he did stick right to my side and keep studying me. I picked up my pace and tried to out walk him.

One minute I was going along fine, and the next, the ground wasn't where it should have been. I fell face first into dried grass because of some kind of animal hole. The impact felt like a punch to my face. Stunned, I lay there for a moment as the smell of copper filled my nose.

I groaned, rolled onto my back, and yipped at the sight of a grey face right in front of mine. Without thinking, I pushed him away then immediately jerked my hand back and covered my face. Nothing happened. I peeked through my fingers and saw him studying my chest again.

"Enough already. Boobs," I said pointing. "They're boobs. And staring doesn't make them go away. I tried."

He tilted his head and pointed at my chest.

"Boob," he said.

I paused mid-nose wipe and stared. He was talking. English.

"Boobs," he said, reaching for one.

I slapped his hand away and sat up.

"No. No more grabbing."

He flexed his hand as he glanced at it then back at me. Too late, I realized what I'd done and stared at him with round eyes. What was I thinking? He'd snapped necks and tossed bodies right in front of me.

"Grabbing boobs."

He reached forward again, and I blocked his hand before it reached its destination.

"Stop."

He cocked his head, eyes narrowing slightly.

"Stop," he repeated.

I licked my lips, and a copper tang bloomed on the tip of my tongue. With a shaky hand, I wiped under my nose. A smear of blood coated my fingers. Crap. I tugged my sleeve over my hand and brought it up to my nose to staunch the bleeding.

With a frown, the creature pulled my hand away from my face. He lifted my sleeve and looked at my wrist. Then he grabbed the other hand and looked at that wrist too before focusing on my nose...my blood. I couldn't move as he leaned forward, his lips curling back over those massive fangs.

Please don't bite me. Please don't bite me.

My silent plea changed abruptly when, nose to nose, he inhaled deeply.

Please find the smell repulsive. Please. Please. Plleeaase.

He pulled back, his gaze locked on mine. My panicked thoughts were still trying to decipher his lack of distinguishable expression when he jerked his gaze from mine and stared at the darkness to our left.

Nothing good had been coming out of the dark since the

sun had set. Zombies. Hellhounds. Him.

A howl sounded from the direction he was looking.

I shivered and debated what to do. Try to run? I glanced at the man-creature squatting beside me. How far would I get? Would it piss him off? Would I fall on my face again?

He stood, and I scooted backwards, trying to get to my feet and failing in my fear. My heart bounced into my throat. I stopped crab crawling backwards, flipped over, and scrambled to my feet.

My captor seemed to have eyes in the back of his head because he'd already moved so he stood in front of me.

"Stop," he said.

Yeah, right. Like I wanted to stay and go toe to toe with one of those hellhounds. Before I could step around him, the sound of paws pounding against the dirt had me pivoting to face the new threat.

Shit. How fast did those beasts move?

A snarl came from the dark ahead and just to the left. Another, slightly to the right, answered the first. I couldn't outrun them. And, I knew what would happen when they found us. My breathing grew choppy, and my muscles wanted to turn to liquid.

My captor stepped around me and crouched low just as I spotted two sets of glowing red eyes speeding toward us. One in front of us and one to the right. The sound of their growls increased. A third rattling growl joined the first two, and I searched the dark, waiting for another set of eyes. When none came, I glanced at the dark back shielding me, realizing the sound was coming from him.

Yards from us, the hounds slowed, their dark bodies just visible in the weak moonlight. Ribs protruded from under their mangy, short fur. Yet, even starved, their long and tall bodies made them look large.

The hellhound in front of us dipped its head low. Saliva dripped from its jowls. The hellhound to the right darted forward, snapping his teeth. I backpedaled and fell. My elbow connected with a rock, and the pain robbed me of air as I watched the hounds make their move.

With its jaws open wide, the hellhound to the right dove straight for my defender's neck. The man lunged forward and caught the hound around the torso. The pair of them fell to the side, struggling. But, I didn't watch their fight. I watched the other hound focused on me. When it tensed, ready to spring, I frantically felt the ground for the rock.

The hound launched itself at me as my fingers closed around my only weapon. Before I could lift my hand, the grey man appeared in front of me with inhuman speed. The hellhound's long, lethal claws tore his shirt as the two collided. With a forearm braced against the beast's throat, he barely avoided the yellowed, snapping teeth. I feared what would happen if the beast bit him.

A noise to my right had me finally scrambling to my feet. The first hellhound was getting up. It looked at the fighting pair then stalked around them as its gaze shifted to me. I shadowed its moves, circling around the opposite way.

I got about a quarter of the way around the fighting pair when the man let out a monstrous bellow. He reached up and caught the snapping hellhound's jaws in his hands. His biceps bulged as he gripped around the beast's mouth and heaved. The lower jaw came away with a spray of blood and wet sound that made me gag.

The other hellhound howled its displeasure. Hefting the weight of the wounded one, the man twisted around and threw one beast into the other. Pinned under the weight of its weakly flailing partner, the hound growled and snapped and struggled to gain its feet.

The man cocked his head at the beast, snarled, then turned toward me.

I backed up as he strode forward. He said a string of words that made no sense. But they sure sounded angry. I kept backing away.

The hellhound was slowly working its way out from under its partner.

"Stop."

My heart almost quit at his command.

"Go," he said.

Before I could figure out what he meant, he grabbed me by my bruised elbow and started walking, pulling me along. I hissed in pain and stumbled as I tried to keep up with him. Although I really wanted to get away from the hellhounds as fast as possible, my legs were definitely not as long as his.

His grip tightened, and he pulled me harder. The throb in my elbow intensified.

"Wait," I panted, trying to tug my arm free.

He grunted and moved in front of me.

I lifted my chin, ready to tell him I was moving as fast as I could when he bent forward, dipped his shoulder, and caught me around the waist. My breath left in a whoosh as his shoulder dug into my soft stomach and he lifted me into the air.

The brute wrapped an arm around my legs and took off running. My hair flew around my head. I opened my mouth to tell him to put me down then reconsidered. The ground whipped past at an incredible speed. Faster than I could ever dream of going. And, there were two hellhounds behind us. Closing my mouth, I grabbed the back of his shirt and hung on.

He ran tirelessly. Around us, the sky began to lighten enough that I could make out the highway in the distance and a few buildings in the other direction.

Eventually, he slowed and then stopped. When he leaned forward to put me on my feet, I groaned with relief. My stomach and head were killing me.

He loosened his hold on me as blood rushed to places it hadn't reached while I rode over his shoulder. Feeling lightheaded, I struggled to find my balance. My legs started to shake, and I began to drop. He caught me by my bruised elbow again. This time I didn't bite back the cry of pain that made my eyes water. He released me slowly and followed my descent down.

He squatted near me and brought his long fingers to rest under my eyes. He dabbed at the wetness and pulled it back to his nose. He closed his eyes as he breathed in.

Exhaustion made me not care that he was sniffing me again.

"Let go," he said suddenly.

"You're going to let me go?"

He frowned then made a bunch of word-sounding noises that were incomprehensible to me.

"Who are you? *What* are you?" I asked.

"Drav."

"I don't know what you're saying."

"Drav," he said, patting his chest again. He didn't try grabbing me. His gaze remained steadily on mine.

"Is that your name?"

"Name Drav."

"Drav," I said slowly. A monster with a name.

He reached forward, clearly aiming for my chest again.

"Boobs."

I crossed my arms over his goals, effectively blocking him.

"No. My name is Mya. Not boobs. And boobs aren't for grabbing."

"My-ah," he repeated

He sat back on his haunches.

"I just want to go home."

Drav's eerie eyes met mine.

"Home," he repeated.

I looked away to the glow on the horizon and hoped the light indicated the direction for Oklahoma City and not someone's yard light. Time to finish this journey, lose my stalker, and get home to my family. I climbed to my feet.

A strong hand wrapped around my bruised elbow. I yelped and tried to pull my arm back. Drav moved in front of me, his large fingers still pressing into my sensitive skin.

"Ow," I said.

Drav trailed his hand down my arm. I winced when he

skimmed over my elbow.

"You can't grab me there. It's bruised."

"Bruised?" He cocked his head and lifted my arm.

Drav's nostrils flared, and his eyes widened. I didn't like the look on the big brute's face, and my pulse jumped in alarm. His gaze fixated on my sleeve. My dried blood dotted the cuff from where I'd wiped my bloody nose.

He bunched the fabric between his fingers and pulled back hard. I stumbled forward, the sound of tearing fabric cutting through the otherwise quiet world around us. I gaped up at him, as he yanked half my sleeve off my arm and held it up in his hand. He growled at the fabric then paced away.

In stunned silence, I watched him quickly dig a hole and toss my sleeve in. Could my life get any weirder?

Shivering at the cool air on my exposed arm, I turned toward the distant glow of Oklahoma City and started walking. In two steps, he was beside me.

We didn't speak as we moved closer and closer to the outlaying north-eastern portion of the city. Very faintly, I heard a quick succession of pops. The noises grew with each passing step. Worry twisted in my stomach. Shots meant infected, hellhounds, more Dravs or all three. I hoped Mom, Dad, and Ryan would be safe.

When the first houses came into sight, Drav slowed. I kept going until he grabbed my arm again.

"Will you please stop yanking on my arms? They're going to fall off," I said in a harsh whisper.

Drav blinked at me then let go.

"Thank you. Next time try saying stop or wait."

He motioned to a copse of trees and nudged me in that direction when I didn't immediately start moving. I looked at the houses and reluctantly gave into his urging. Some of the lights were on, some weren't. Who knew what lurked inside. Infected? Scared humans with guns? Both would be dangerous.

In the shadow of the trees, he watched the houses. I shifted my weight from foot to foot and yawned until my eyes watered. He kept glancing at me but didn't say anything.

As we stood there, I realized the kind of decisions that lay before me. Life or death ones. I'd always thought the saying, "or die trying" sounded so melodramatic. But now it was my reality.

Sitting heavily, I leaned against the trunk of the nearest tree.

Was I smart to keep trying to get home? I didn't know. I didn't see any safer option. If I stayed in the trees, one of those hounds would find me eventually. Or the infected. I listened to the pop, pop, pop and decided, at least in the city, I might pick up a gun. Or die trying.

I shivered and closed my eyes as I thought about what waited for me.

Hellhounds, zombies, demon looking man-people who liked breaking necks and ripping off jaws...I was so fucked.

SEVEN

Something tickled my neck, and I awoke with a gasp. The night sky had lightened with the approaching dawn, and the air no longer rang with distant pops. In fact, an eerie silence blanketed the area, including the vacant space before me where Drav had stood.

I turned my head to check the trees to my left for him and almost screamed. Drav blinked at me, just inches away, then stood from his squatted position.

Taking a deep breath to calm my racing heart, I looked down at myself. I didn't know what I expected. Blood? Wounds? Signs of a recent groping? To my surprise, I found Drav's dark shirt covering me. I touched the warm material and looked up at him as he stepped away to watch the houses once more.

I sat for a moment, confused as hell. Nothing about Drav made sense. Standing, I winced at the pressure on my bladder. How long had I slept? Maybe an hour? Two? And he'd watched over me. Why? I shook my head, unable to believe I'd slept at all.

With his shirt in my hands, I cautiously approached him. He looked down at me, his gaze sweeping over my face and hair as I held out his shirt.

"Thank you," I said.

He studied me for a moment longer before he took the shirt with a grunt of acknowledgement. He tugged the shirt over his head then went back to watching the houses.

Since he didn't show any sign of wanting to leave soon, the need to pee had me glancing back at the trees again. The inky shadows had me questioning how badly I needed to go. Bad enough to seriously consider dropping my pants where I stood. I looked at Drav and knew that wasn't an option, given his previous crotch groping and interest in my boobs.

Scrubbing my hands over my face, I turned toward the trees. He stood in front of me before I took a second step. I looked up at him. He blinked at me.

"I have to pee," I said.

He didn't move.

"If I go stand behind a tree, is something going to attack me? My loose use of 'something' includes you."

He blinked at me again.

"I don't like when you do that."

He didn't blink, which freaked me out more.

"How much of what I say do you understand?"

He turned away from me and walked into the trees a few feet, making me think he didn't understand much at all. He looked back and motioned for me to follow.

"I don't want to leave. I want to go home." I pointed to the nearest house. "I just wanted to pee, first."

"You pee. No attack. Includes me."

My mouth dropped open. When he'd repeated boob and grab, I'd thought he'd just parroted the words.

"No leave. Go home," he said.

He moved toward me, and I backed up a step, my heart hammering. He understood me. Not only understood me, but what he'd just said almost made it sound like he would take me home. That couldn't be right. Yet, unlike my previous companions, I still lived. I opened my mouth to ask if he really meant that he would help me get home, but that didn't come out.

"Why did you kill Kevin and Josh? And probably Russ? Are you going to kill me? Where did you come from? Why are you here? What is happening?"

He frowned. "No."

"No? Those weren't 'no' questions."

"No leave. Go home. You pee."

"Can you at least tell me what's happening?"

"Pee."

He stood before me, a solid mass of authority. He didn't need to cross his arms to make that point either.

"Yeah, yeah, yeah. I know pee. Fine. But, I can't pee with you staring at me. It's creepy. If it's safe, go back to watching the houses." I didn't trust his perverse curiosity.

He moved back into his watchful position. I hurried to a nearby tree and unbuttoned my pants, but before I tugged my pants down, I debated. Face him to make sure he didn't peek or the woods so I wasn't attacked with my pants down? I scooted over so the tree would hopefully block his view. I faced the woods, squatted, and power peed like my life depended on it.

When I finished, I zipped up and tried not to think about

the grossness. The world was ending, and I had bigger problems than no toilet paper.

I turned and found Drav looking my direction. As I joined him, I didn't acknowledge the fact he'd probably tried to sneak a peek. Thankfully, the few houses nearest the trees where we hid had no lights shining.

"My home is on the other side of the city," I said, still unsure what he could understand.

When he didn't answer, I sighed and studied the houses before us.

"What's smarter? Cutting through or going around? Cutting through might mean running into infected. But, it could also mean water, food…" I stopped thinking aloud when I realized the other reason I wanted to cut through instead of going around. I wanted to find the humans with the guns I'd heard. I glanced at Drav, wondering what would happen then, and found him watching me, his head slightly tilted.

Crap. I shouldn't have mentioned food. I really hoped I didn't look like his idea of a steak breakfast.

Pretending like I hadn't just unnerved myself, I made the decision and took a step forward.

"If we see any infected, you have my permission to toss me over your shoulder and run."

He didn't try to stop me as I crept toward another grouping of trees closer to the houses. When I reached them, I checked for the next bit of protective cover. Slowly, dash by mad-dash, I made my way into the first of many subdivisions.

The neighborhood appeared unnaturally quiet. With the sun almost kissing the horizon, there should have been kids up, getting ready for school, parents leaving to go to work. Movement. Noise. Something. Instead, there was the whisper of wind rattling the few dry leaves still clinging to otherwise barren branches and the snap of a sheet that billowed in the wind. I glanced at the white material caught in the window and my stomach tightened with worry. Everything seemed so desolate.

The further we scurried, the quieter it got. Not even the occasional bark of someone's dog reached our ears.

I saw the first infected after three blocks of traveling. Before I could react, Drav pulled me behind a tree. With a hammering heart, I waited as a man in sweatpants and t-shirt shambled up the center of the street, his bare feet dragging on the pavement with a rasp. The sound burrowed into my mind. Crsht. Crsht. The need to cover my ears made me twitch. Drav's hand brushed over my back, a weird comfort that gave me courage to keep watching the infected's progress.

The infected man could have passed as a sleep walker if not for the bites on his arm. He didn't turn his head to look around or veer from his ambling path down the center of the road. Drawing a deep breath after he passed from sight, I prepared to dash to the next tree then saw the bloody trail he'd left behind. A shiver chased through me, and I forced myself to focus on reaching the next area of cover.

Sightings became more frequent as the sun rose to show a beautiful, clear blue November sky. I doubted the sun had anything to do with the amount of infected drifting around. Those numbers likely had everything to do with the increase of houses.

When I moved to dash to the next form of cover, a car in a driveway, Drav put his hand on my shoulder and stopped me. I glanced at him, and my eyes widened in surprise at the sight of his tearing eyes. For a moment, I thought he was crying.

"No," he said softly.

He blinked profusely, the light making his eyes water as he looked around. Before I could ask why he'd said no, he grabbed the side of my shirt and tugged me back the way we'd come.

The sudden and rapid *pop, pop, pop* not far away made me jump. Drav didn't mess around with more tugging. He flipped me over his shoulder and took off running. When he lurched upward and the distance between my head and the ground tripled, I almost screamed.

A second later, we landed on the inside of a fence. He didn't stop moving. Something cracked and we were suddenly inside someone's kitchen. He set me on my feet and turned to push the door shut. It didn't latch since he'd busted the bolt right through the jamb. I reached around him to use the security chain.

Outside the pops continued, a sign of people nearby. People with guns, who could possibly help me get home. Humans.

I started moving toward the living room at the front of the house, but Drav snagged me again and spun me around.

"No."

"But there's—"

"No," he said more forcefully.

I swallowed any further objection. When I stayed silent,

he seemed to calm slightly and began to look around the room. I did, too. Items from pulled out drawers lay scattered everywhere. The people had either left in a hurry or their home had been looted.

I glanced down the hall at all the closed doors.

"Are we safe in here?" I whispered.

Drav nudged me toward the hall, and I hoped that meant yes. At the end of the hall, he turned and sat, blocking me in at the back.

"What are you doing?"

He laid his head back against the wall and closed his eyes.

"Uh…" I waited for him to do something more, but he didn't. He just stayed there.

The noises outside remained consistent, neither moving closer nor fading. My ticket home couldn't be more than a block or two away. I just needed to get past Drav, sneak out a broken door, hop a six-foot fence…shit. Front door then. I'd need to watch the front yard and street before even thinking about opening the door.

First, I'd have to cross over Drav. The hall wasn't wide so his bent knees created a barrier for what would have been an easy step. His wide shoulders and overall largeness didn't help either. I moved a little, making a slight noise to test him. His eyes remained closed. I lifted my foot and was halfway over him when his fingers closed around the ankle of my anchored foot. I yipped in surprise and almost fell on him before my other foot landed hard on the other side of him. He slowly tipped his head up at me and opened one eye.

"No."

The soft way he said the word made me shiver.

"I-I was just going to look for food. I'm h-hungry."

Drav tilted his head at me and released my ankle. He nudged me back as he stood up. He didn't move away, but stared down at me with very little space between us. When he leaned in and inhaled near my hair, I swallowed hard and hoped he wouldn't somehow detect the lie.

Finally, he stepped back and motioned that I could go. I retreated down the hall and went to the kitchen. The fridge still hummed, and I checked inside of it. Nothing remained but condiments. I checked the cupboards next. They'd been cleared out, too, except for some cans of peaches. I grabbed one then started looking for a can opener. The first drawer I opened had odds and ends and a pair of sunglasses.

"Look," I said, holding them up. He blinked at the pink and bedazzled frames. "They'll cover your eyes so the light doesn't hurt. Like this." I put them on then took them off and handed them to him. "If you wear them, we can go back outside. I can go home."

He looked them over then set them on the counter.

"No." He opened the next drawer. "Hungry."

With frustration, I searched the contents of that drawer, too. Finding the can opener, I opened the can and poured the peaches into a clean bowl. He closely observed everything I did. I stabbed a peach half with a fork and took a bite.

"Are you hungry?" I asked after I swallowed. Gathering my courage, and hoping like hell he didn't say "people," I asked, "What do you eat?"

He stole the fork from my hand and ate the rest of the

peach.

"Uh…okay." Peaches were good. Much better than people.

Once I finished eating, though, he herded me back down the hall.

"You sure you don't want to try those sunglasses?"

"No." He sat in his same spot and closed his eyes.

This time, I sat as well. He hadn't left me much room. I wedged myself between him and the wall and sighed. My phone dug into my butt, a silent comfort. Temptation prodded me to check it, but I didn't want to bring it to Drav's attention. Instead, I closed my eyes and forced myself to relax. Hopefully, he'd been awake longer than I had before my nap. And, I hoped the little bit of sleep I'd gotten would be enough to keep me awake until he fell asleep. While I waited, I imagined the yards we'd crossed, the direction of the shots, and the cover I might find between here and there.

After a few minutes, my thoughts began drifting to what I would do once I reached home. What if my family had been infected? Where would I go? What was left in the world? Did we, the uninfected humans have any chance of surviving? How many hellhounds prowled out there? How many humans had already been infected? There was only one way to learn. I had to go explore. I had to find the people shooting and figure out what happened. I had to know my family was safe.

EIGHT

I waited a long time. The shots started to fade. Several times, I caught myself on the verge of dozing off. The last time, I twitched and knew I had to try, now or never. I opened my eyes and observed Drav for several minutes. He had closed his eyes and leaned his head back against the wall. He seemed asleep.

Taking my time, I got to my feet. If he caught me again, I'd say I had to pee. However, this time, he didn't move.

Carefully, I made my way down the hallway and to the front door. I looked through the window, scanning the street, then slipped outside.

My nerves stretched tight as I sprinted to the first bit of cover. Alert for infected, hellhounds, and, possibly, a killer shadow man, I bolted for the next bit of cover. Sprint by sprint, I made my way south-west, further into the city. Tracking the shooters wasn't hard. They'd left a trail of dead infected bodies. However, the gun shots attracted more infected to the area, too.

A few times, I thought one spotted me. However, the infected never ran after me like they had on the road. The more I saw, the more I began seeing patterns. They shambled fairly directionless until they heard something. Then they ran toward the sound, but their speed only lasted for short bursts. So, if one heard me, I would need to quietly out distance it to avoid attracting more.

The gun fire grew louder around lunch, and I spotted the shooter. He stood by his truck, which idled at an intersection. The gun in his hands remained aimed down the road to the left. Knowing better than to call out, I waved my arms in the air to get his attention.

"There's a live one out there," I heard someone else call. "Ten o'clock."

Every infected between me and the shooter dropped, one right after another, gunned down before the man by the truck turned toward me. Movement near a chimney to the right drew my attention, and I looked up at a man dressed in brown and black. Blonde hair stuck out from his black beanie.

"I've got you," he called. "Get to the truck."

I didn't need to be told twice. I sprinted toward the truck, my shoes thumping against the blacktop. The shooter on the ground, dressed in the same black and brown clothing as the man on the roof, waved me past. A single shot rang out behind me.

I opened the back door of the huge pickup truck and climbed in. Behind the wheel sat a third man dressed similarly to the other two. I quickly shut the door as he scanned the area around the truck.

"Hey," I said, a little winded from the mad dash.

He continued to ignore me. I anxiously glanced out the window and tried to calm my racing heart.

No more pops sounded in the distance. Nervous, elated

DEMON EMBER

energy buzzed in my veins. Finding more humans, alive ones, was huge. They had guns and appeared military. I started to relax in my seat. I'd done it. I'd made it. I wanted to grin.

Static crackled from a hand radio before a voice came through.

"Jack's down from the roof. He said he spotted one of the big grey ones in the distance."

My grin faded. Images of the last time I rode in a truck flashed through my head. No, I thought. Not again. I frantically looked out the windows as the driver pulled the radio from the cup-holder.

"Got it," he said into the radio. "Girl is in the truck. Get your asses back here."

The door opened to my left, and I scooted over the bench as the man from the ground climbed in the back with me.

"Where did you come from?" he asked.

"Tulsa. I was at school."

His eyes swept over me as Jack, the blonde man from the roof, climbed into the front seat.

"Moving out," the driver called as he put the vehicle into gear. The engine revved as the truck started forward in a rush. Jack laughed, twisted around, and offered his hand over the seat.

"You surprised me," he said. "Very nice to meet you, ma'am."

I gave him a weak smile and shook his hand. After I released it, he turned forward and rolled his window down, his gun ready. The truck began picking up speed, but not enough. I knew how fast the shadow men could run. I looked out the back window, my gaze searching.

"What's your name, girl?" the man beside me asked. I met his tired brown gaze and noted the subtle wrinkles around his eyes.

"Mya."

"I'm Charles, that's Bill driving, and Jack up front."

"What were you saying about a big grey one?"

"Damn demons that control the hellhounds," Bill said from the front.

"What?" Hellhound-controlling demons? My stomach lurched.

"Wait until you see one. Then you'll know. Hell's rising, kid."

The image of Drav fighting off the hellhounds flashed through my mind. He certainly didn't control those hounds. They had attacked us. And he protected me from them. Did it really matter? I was finally in a moving vehicle in my home city.

I opened my mouth to ask more questions when a boom from Jack's gun filled the cab. I slammed my hands over my ears and turned in my seat to look out the window. Another infected started an all-out sprint toward us.

Jack fired again. I flinched as the bullet tore through the infected man's chest and knocked him backwards. Instead of going down, he still kept coming. Jack took another two shots, the last finally going through the infected's head. I cringed as he crumbled to the ground.

"First time seeing one die?" Charles asked quietly.

He held his gun steadily out the window, too. I had no

experience with guns but still wished I had my own.

I slowly shook my head to answer his question. No matter how many I saw die, I doubted I'd ever forget the infected had once been a person.

"What happened here? My phone doesn't work," I said, pulling it from my back pocket.

"Don't bother," he said as I checked for new messages. "We've lost communications. First, the tremors, then communications, then the hounds. Most folks were in their houses for the night when the first wave of mutts came through the city. They didn't know what was happening out on the streets."

"What was happening?" I asked, even though I had a fairly good idea.

"Those hounds attacked anything that was out. Some people they killed. Some they bit then moved on. Alive or dead, didn't matter. The people bitten all got sick, and the sickness spread like wildfire throughout the night. Tinker started to mobilize an evacuation effort around two," Charles said, referring to the military base in Oklahoma City. "But, people didn't understand what was going on. As soon as they left their houses, they came into contact with neighbors, friends, and family that had been infected. One bite and they were done for."

Jack fired another shot, and a shudder ran through me. Would my family have tried to leave? Would I find them shambling around our neighborhood?

"What happened then?"

"We helped get as many uninfected civilians as we could

back to base. They started flying out survivors to a fenced in location further north."

"Why are you guys still here?" I asked.

"This is home. We're not giving up on it. While we gather supplies and search for stragglers like you, we're clearing the infected. If we could manage to kill the hounds and their masters, we'd get our city back."

I remembered the way the hellhound had kept going even after being shot at the stadium.

"Have you killed any?"

"Hounds?"

I nodded.

"Not sure. They take off when we put a few rounds in them. I'm hoping that means they die somewhere."

"Those grey bastards are a different story," Jack said without taking his eyes from the passing houses.

"Why?"

"You don't see them," Charles said. "They are shadows that leave bodies behind. We only know they exist because we caught two on surveillance. Looked like a couple big men at first. The footage was blurry. We watched them take down seven armed soldiers. Shots were fired but never seemed to hit either one. We thought it was the shadows making their skin grey but learned the truth when one faced the direction of the camera. Its eyes weren't human."

No, Drav's eyes were far from human. And it terrified me that there were more of them out there.

"So it's just the three of you out looking for survivors?"

Jack laughed from up front.

"We're one of many units," he said, giving me hope. "After Tinker mobilized, we lost more than half. But we're still here."

The truck stayed quiet for a moment except for the dull roar of the engine and random bangs from the gun.

"Have you found anyone else?" I asked hopefully. "I'm looking for my family."

"You're the first we've run into. We have been out since dawn. But we were double-checking an area already evaced. Where did you live?"

The past-tense way he said it made my stomach cramp.

"Blueridge. North-west side," I said.

"We'll make sure someone goes out that way to check for signs of life today."

"What do you mean signs of life?"

"People hang sheets outside windows or doors. Some have painted help in their windows. Makes it easier for us to find them and, hopefully, get them to safety," Charles explained.

"Can't we check my neighborhood now?"

"We have orders to go further into the city for supplies," Charles said.

"Roll them up," Bill said from the front as he slowed for a turn.

"Did you really just use your blinker?" Jack asked, pulling his gun in and rolled up his window.

"Shut up."

Jack laughed, and I glanced at Charles who'd pulled his gun in, too, and frowned.

"Why are we rolling up the windows?"

"We're taking the highway," Jack said. "Splatter control."

As soon as we turned again, I saw the highway ahead. In the distance, infected shambled along the road.

"Why are there so many?"

"Failed attempt at a ground-evac."

"Here we go," Bill said, taking the ramp.

Bill's hands tightened on the wheel, and the engine roared to life as he pressed down on the gas. The roar announced our location to the infected. They came running at the truck. My stomach knotted. Bill aimed right for them. Half of one's body flew over the truck. More came at us like a swarm of gnats. Bill plowed through them all. I shut my eyes unable to erase the image of the blood that spattered the windshield.

The squeak of the window-wipers sounded then finally stopped.

"We clean up more of them every run," Charles said.

Slowly, I opened my eyes.

Jack leaned over in his seat and turned the volume nob up on the radio. Only static crackled out. He switched over to the tune nob, and twisted it around. A high-pitched screech emitted from a station that should have been playing rock. After Jack tried a couple more stations, Bill reached over and turned the radio button off.

"Has there been any news of what's happening anywhere else?" I asked.

"No. The last I heard, Europe had gone dark just after the local news stations reported sightings of those demonic hounds."

Yesterday afternoon. It had only been that long since the first tremor, since Germany fell with the same sickness. Yet it felt like I had lived a hundred years in those few hours.

I looked out the window at the quiet neighborhoods and occasional infected as we continued down the highway.

After taking an exit, the number of zombies thinned for a while. However, the closer we got to downtown, the more they came out. Jack and Charles shot out their open windows as Bill drove. The shots didn't deter any away from us. Instead, it did the opposite. More started to filter out, beckoned by the noise, and I began to rethink my itch to possess a gun of my own.

It wasn't much longer until we arrived at a shopping district.

"Bill, you keep the path between the truck and the store clear," Charles said. "The rest of us are going for the food and water. Take carts. Get everything you can."

"Me?" I didn't want to leave the safety of the truck.

"These supplies are going with you to the survivor camp. You want to eat, don't you?"

I nodded.

"We'll keep you safe. Just grab a cart and get as many canned and dry goods as you can. Use the radios. I want to be gone in fifteen."

Bill drove the truck around the back of a supermarket and killed the engine. The infected that had chased us slowed to a confused shamble in the quiet. We sat in the truck for twenty minutes, watching and waiting for the infected to slowly disperse.

Charles called all clear, and we went to the employee entrance, where Jack picked the lock.

"Quieter this way," he said softly when he caught me watching.

As soon as the door opened, Jack lifted his gun and stepped inside. Someone had left the lights on in the back room. Pallets of boxes sat just inside the large delivery doors to our right.

I pointed, but Charles shook his head.

"Too big."

Charles nodded toward the swinging door that led to the main shopping area. Jack checked the window then eased the door open. I slowly followed him through. Everything seemed quietly undisturbed. Charles motioned for us to stay. My stomach churned as I watched him walk away and disappear around the corner of an aisle.

A few minutes later, a couple of pops echoed through the store, and I jumped.

"Store cleared," Charles said softly over the radio.

Jack jerked his head to the left then started moving. I followed him to the front of the store. The instant scratch off machine had been pushed in front of the door. Bits of glass covered the floor around it.

"Hellhounds," Jack said softly.

"Here?" I asked, my panic going through the roof.

He shook his head. "Here and gone again. They move fast."

Exactly why I didn't want to be in a building with them.

"Get a cart," he said, holstering his gun. We each grabbed

a cart and started for the shelves. Another few pops echoed, but from outside.

"Took out two infected. Keep your eyes open," Bill said over the radio.

Jack went ahead of me and started sweeping the nearest shelf of the nonperishable foods. We filled both carts and went to the water aisle next. Jack grabbed an abandoned cart and started loading the gallon jugs.

Another pop sounded from outside.

"Head back to the car now," Bill barked over the radio. Jack grabbed the food cart and hustled for the employee door.

"Grey one headed right for us. Get out, now."

"Shit." Jack spun around.

"What do we do?" I panted.

"Get out before it gets here. Leave the cart."

He grabbed my arm and started running toward the back. I struggled to keep up. Fear solidified in my stomach.

"Bill left the keys in the truck. Get it started. I'm almost there," Charles said through the radio.

We had nearly reached the employee entrance when a scream ripped through the air. I faltered, but Jack didn't pause in his running. He pulled me through the exit. I stumbled, blinded by the sudden sunlight.

Jack kept pulling me, and I squinted as I followed after him. The truck waited, only steps away.

Suddenly Jack's hand left my arm. I blinked, looking around in confusion.

When I turned a full circle, I saw Jack's body slumped against the truck, his neck bent unnaturally. Standing over him was a very pissed off Drav.

NINE

His shoulders heaved with each angry breath as he stalked toward me. I shook with fear, unable to tear my gaze from the pink bedazzled sunglasses he wore. When he stood before me, he leaned down until his eyes were level with mine.

"Arm fall off."

The deep, quiet words turned my fear to confusion.

"W-what?"

He reached out and stroked one finger along my bruised elbow. The same arm Jack had just been tugging on.

"Get down!" Charles bellowed from somewhere behind me.

Drav roared in my face, put his shoulder to my stomach, and hoisted me into the air. An arm around my thighs anchored me. As he turned, I braced my arms on his back and lifted my head. Charles stood by the door, rifle poised and ready to fire. Our eyes met. His hopeless, sad expression ratcheted my panic higher, and I struggled in Drav's hold.

A large hand came down on my ass with a loud crack. I forgot to struggle as I choked on a pained squeal. Drav took off running.

"Sorry, kid," Charles said.

A moment later, a loud bang filled the air. Stunned, I

stared at Charles as he took aim again. He'd actually pulled the trigger. I cried out and tucked myself close to Drav's torso, wrapping my arms around his waist as he ran.

Another shot rang out. My heart wanted to pound its way out through my throat. Drav jerked but didn't slow. Blacktop, interspersed with flashes of green, continued to pass underneath me at an alarming rate. My hair whipped around my head. Even when the shots stopped, Drav didn't.

I loosened my hold on his waist and lifted my head. His arm tightened on the backs of my thighs and a hand settled on my sore butt cheek. That was all the warning I needed to resume my clinging position.

What I'd glimpsed had been enough. Infected trailed behind us, attracted by the sound of the shots and Drav's running. Although he outpaced them, I didn't want to know if one came close or if their numbers grew. If Drav wanted me to hold still so he could run, I would. And, I wouldn't think about what would happen when he stopped running or about the way he'd roared in my face. Nope. I'd cling to him like a second skin and think of how I would make it home and how we'd all go somewhere safe.

Charles had said they'd evacuated people to a location somewhere north of the city. I regretted not asking where and tried to focus on the positive bits of information I knew. An evacuation had occurred. People were safely flown away to a fenced in location. Fences had to be good. Especially if they were military. So, if my family was there—wherever there might be—they would be safe. I had to believe that. But, first, I needed to make sure they had actually been evacuated and weren't with the stragglers Charles had mentioned.

Drav jumped, startling me from my thoughts, and I looked down to see a fence pass under us. Another fenced in yard, proving my thought that fences were good. I heard the wood crack as he broke in through the back door. Finally, he set me on my feet.

For a moment, I wobbled unsteadily as the blood rushed from my head. Drav set his sunglasses on the counter then gently touched my shoulder. I fearfully met his gaze.

Before I could ponder what he would do to me, a whisper of noise came from our left. Drav spun toward the sound and crouched low in front of me. A man, his eyes lifelessly cloudy, rushed toward us.

I gasped and my fight or flight instinct surged. I would have run, but to where? A stupid fenced in backyard? I was a fish in a barrel.

Drav waited until the man came close, then lashed out, ripping the head clear from the body in one powerful swing. Dark, clotted blood spattered the wall behind the man. I gagged and closed my eyes.

"Mya."

The sound of my name made me wince.

"Mya. Eyes. Look me."

I opened my eyes and found him standing before me once more. The decapitated infected lay on the floor behind him. Would I be next? Was that why he'd come after me and killed the rest of Charles's group?

Nerves pushed too far, I trembled uncontrollably and numbly stared up at Drav. His gaze swept over my face as if he was checking for something. What, I had no idea. The heavy exhale he released made me jump. The way he reached around me to grab the back of my head made my heart hammer. I closed my eyes, waiting for the end. Instead, his forehead pressed against mine and his breath fanned my face.

Surprised, I opened my eyes. The up-close view of his eyes startled me less than the feel of his fingers gently massaging my scalp.

He stayed like that for a moment before slowly straightening. His gaze held mine as he lightly ran his fingers along my hair. When his fingers reached the ends, he brought the long strands to his nose. With growing nervousness, I watched him inhale deeply. He killed a lot. People. Hellhounds. Infected. But not me. And, the potential reason why terrified me.

Releasing my hair, he turned to look at the fallen body. He grunted at it, as if annoyed, then reached down to pick it and the head up.

"Mya, no go back outside."

I nodded slightly.

He stepped around me, and I watched him carry the infected to the back of the fence then chuck both the body and the head over. The early morning sun caught on the face as the head tumbled down. Was this my life? Death and hiding and fear?

Drav turned, and his watery gaze never left mine as he stalked back across the yard. I stepped aside, hoping he would pass me, but he shadowed my move, crowding into my space.

"I'm sorry, Mya."

Was he just repeating Charles' words or was he really sorry for stealing me?

He glanced at the dark hallway then nudged me in that direction. This time, the doors weren't closed. The sight of the first clean, cozy bed reminded me how very little sleep I had gotten. Until now, adrenaline had kept my exhaustion away. However, that was fading fast.

When I saw a bathroom, I stopped.

"Mya." Drav's tone held a note of warning.

"I want to pee," I said. I didn't. Not really. I wanted to climb my ass out that big window and see if I could run my way back to Charles or some other humans.

He grunted and nudged me toward the bathroom. When I stepped in and tried to close the door, he blocked it.

"No."

"I'm not peeing with you watching me."

He turned and looked at the mirror.

"Not helpful. Leave," I said.

"No. Mya leave." He looked at the window, and I swallowed hard.

"Out the window?" I said, feigning disbelief. "I would never fit."

"You would fit," he said.

Not sure what to say to that, I went to the sink and turned on the water, unwilling to make it obvious that he'd correctly busted me. Before I bent to drink, I glanced at myself in the mirror. A smear of dirt decorated the bridge of my nose and one cheek. Crusted bits of blood clung to the skin under my nose.

Changing my mind about the drink, I opened the bathroom closet, grabbed a washcloth, and washed my face. Afterwards, I quenched my thirst and turned off the water.

When I turned toward Drav, I noticed a wet spot on his shirt.

"I think you got a little bit of blood on you," I said, pointing.

He looked down at the spot on his side and then lifted his shirt. A gash split his skin just over his lower ribs.

A bullet had grazed him. I glanced at his shoulder and realized it had been the side on which he'd carried me. My head would have been about right where that bullet had gotten him. My eyes widened as I realized Charles had been aiming for me, not Drav.

"Holy shit," I said softly.

I met Drav's gaze as the implications settled in my mind. Whatever Charles had seen on that video had been enough for him to think I would be better off dead by his hand than Drav's. The questions I'd tried to avoid thinking forced their way in. Why was I still alive? What did Drav plan to do with me?

"D-do you want to clean it?" I asked, instead.

I didn't wait for an answer but grabbed a new washcloth and wet it. He still had his shirt up when I turned back to him, so I held out the washcloth.

"No. You clean it."

He stared at me unblinkingly, unnerving me further. With a shaking hand, I bent forward and began to gently clean the blood away. Drav's free hand went to my hair, his fingers trailing through the strands. I didn't understand his fascination with me, but it had kept me alive so far.

When I finished, I moved away from his inquisitive fingers and grabbed the first aid kit I'd noticed on the shelf. He held still as I put butterfly bandages on the gash. Finished, I straightened away from him and he lowered his shirt.

He waited while I washed my hands then nudged me down the hall again. Instead of sitting on the floor, he steered me toward a small bedroom with closed curtains. In the dim light, the pink and white frilly decor did nothing to cheer me.

"I don't want to sleep on a bed. We can sit in the hallway."

"No. You sleep on the bed," he said, closing the door.

He nudged me toward the bed in question, and my mind raced. Would I now find out why Charles wanted to shoot me? Is this why Drav came back for me?

When I didn't immediately jump onto the bed once we reached it, he picked me up and set me on the soft mattress.

"I don't want to sit here." My voice shook like crazy. So did my hands.

He placed a palm on my chest, just above my thundering heart, and steadily pushed me down until I lay flat on the bed. With wide-eyed panic, I stared up at him. He lowered himself beside me, pulled me into his arms, and buried his nose in my hair. My heart beat so painfully hard and fast that I struggled to breathe.

It took several moments to realize he hadn't moved. I held still and tried to quiet my booming heart so I could hear his slow and steady breathing. Was he really sleeping?

I lifted my head slightly.

"No, Mya. Sleep," he said.

He reached up and gently ran his fingers over my face. When he found my eyes, he swiped over them again and again until I kept them closed.

He grunted and wrapped his arm around me. Despite everything, his hold began to feel safe, not confining. I exhaled heavily.

It didn't take long for my body to agree with him, and I slept.

*   *   *   *

I opened my eyes to a darker version of the room. Comfortable on my side, I could have easily gone back to sleep for another hour, but the very warm hand cupping my left breast posed a problem. Behind me, Drav lay close, with the offending arm curled over my side. We were far too cozy.

Laying still, I listened to his even breathing then carefully pushed at his forearm to remove his hand. His fingers clutched a little tighter around his prize, and he moved closer, his breath tickling the back of my neck. A roller coaster started in my stomach and freaked me out.

"Drav, stop."

He grunted, let go, and sat up. I quickly sat up, too. He was right there, in front of me in the dark, not giving me any room to leave.

"Mya, hungry?"

"Yes." Anything to get out of bed.

"Yeeessss," he drew out the word and something about his tone made me think he was smiling.

"Yes, Mya. Yes, hungry. Yes, home. Yes." He stepped back, giving me some room.

"Uh…okay." I stood and let him guide me to the kitchen. The back yard light shone through the window and illuminated the space well enough to see.

This time he searched for the cans while I checked the fridge. I found a pizza box containing four slices.

"You can stop looking. We can eat this," I said.

I took a slice and set the box on the counter. He watched me take a bite then grabbed a slice and brought it to his mouth. He bit into the pizza, chewed, then spit it onto the floor.

I laughed before I caught myself.

"What's wrong?" I asked. "It's cold, but it's not bad. Don't you like it?"

"No." He went back to searching cupboards and produced a can of spaghetti sauce.

"You sure you want to eat that?" I asked, when he started looking through the drawers. He paused and stared at me.

"It's spaghetti sauce. It's close to the red stuff on the pizza you just spit out."

He grunted, set the can opener on the counter, and went back to the cupboards. Each can he found, he held up to me until I identified it. When he'd emptied the cupboards, he said my name and pointed to the cans.

"You want me to pick?"

"Yes."

I lifted the can of chicken and the can of fruit cocktail. "If you like meat, eat this one. If you like fruit, like we had last time, eat this one."

He took both from me, and I watched him pick up the can opener and open the cans without hesitation. Using his fingers, he picked out some chicken and some fruit and popped both into his mouth at once. He seemed to enjoy it. I took another bite of my pizza and watched as he ate it all and drank the juice left in the fruit can.

I took a glass from the cupboard and filled it with water, drinking three glasses before setting it down. My stomach felt tight, but I didn't know when I'd get food or water next. Drav picked up my glass and proceeded to turn the tap on and off without filling anything.

"While you're doing that, I'm going to use the bathroom."

He looked at me without blinking.

"Pee?" I said.

"Don't leave, Mya."

The progression of his speech and understanding continued to unnerve me.

"I won't leave. Please don't watch me. It's weird."

He didn't try to follow, and I hesitated at the bathroom door. He still watched me.

"I'm going to close the door," I said.

"No." He took a step toward me.

"Fine. I'll leave it open if you promise to stay right there."

He stopped moving. Taking that as an agreement, I turned and quickly stepped into the bathroom. Although the window tempted me, the darkness beyond did not. I decided I would wait and try to find a way to slip from Drav once the sun rose.

Finished using the bathroom, I stepped back into the hall and found Drav in the same spot by the kitchen sink. As soon as he saw me, he turned his attention back to the faucet. Had he really stared at the hallway, listening the whole time? My cheeks grew hot. Too busy getting a drink for himself, he thankfully didn't notice.

TEN

After he drained the glass and set it aside, he looked me over. Not in a creepy way like when we'd first met, but more of a "are you ready?" kind of way. He confirmed that guess by heading toward the front door.

"Mya and Drav go outside," he said quietly.

I watched him wrap his hand around the knob and knew what would happen if he tore the door open. The noise would attract any nearby infected.

"Wait. I can open it," I said, hurrying to him.

He let go of the knob but didn't step aside. I pretended not to notice the way he leaned in to smell my hair as he watched me unlock the bolt then turn the knob.

"Yes," he said, carefully moving me out of the way again so he could open the door and leave first.

He didn't go far. His back blocked the opening as he scanned right to left.

After a moment, he reached back for me. It terrified me to have to step out into the night, knowing what waited in the dark. But, thoughts of my family gave me courage enough to lead the way as Drav and I sprinted for the first bit of cover.

The sound of his soft footfalls behind me eased some of the terror. As much as I worried about what he wanted with me, I also realized how relieved I felt that I wasn't trying to make my way home alone. Bit by bit we moved through one neighborhood to the next, making progress.

I dashed across a quiet street and ducked behind a car in someone's front yard to wait for Drav. A sound had me looking up as a woman came around the side of the house. Fear lanced through me at the sight of her. I could see bite marks through the tears in her bloody shirt. Infected. A small sound escaped me.

Her head jerked in my direction, her mouth opening and closing. She lunged at me, and a solid wall of grey-muscled Drav stepped in front of me. He growled low and caught her by the head.

This time, I shut my eyes. Even without the visual, the wet sounds and the soft thump made bile rise to my throat.

A gentle pressure on my forehead had me opening my eyes. Drav's forehead rested against mine.

"I promise Mya stay safe," he said.

His steady gaze held me, and looking into his odd eyes, I realized what he meant by those words. Drav would keep me safe from the infected. But who would keep me safe from him?

"Thank you," I whispered.

"Yes."

He moved back a little but stayed crouched beside me as I watched the houses and decided the next stop. Avoiding the infected who shambled along the roads posed little issue with a bit of stealth and patience. However, as the woman had just proven, they didn't all stick to open areas.

It took hours before I found myself in an area I actually recognized. During that time, we were discovered by an infected on six different occasions. Drav kept each one away from me. He also removed every head.

"We're not even halfway across town," I said quietly as we stood in the darkness between two houses.

Drav didn't say anything in return, just watched the street and yards before us. I wasn't sure how far he'd run with me, but I felt sure he'd covered more distance with me on his shoulder than we had by doing this duck and cover thing. Only the knowledge that he'd have no idea which direction to go kept me from telling him to carry me again. That meant we would need to keep traveling as we were, and it would be well after dawn before I reached my neighborhood.

Unwilling to give up, I selected the next target and sprinted toward it, Drav right beside me.

Near dawn, he tugged my shirt while we watched the street from behind a parked car.

"Mya, don't go outside," he said softly.

Since I already crouched outside, I had no idea what he meant. I began to understand, though, when he looked at a house with a fenced in yard further down the block. No sheets or paint indicated anyone needing help. Unlike some of the other houses, the front door and garage were closed. It would be a perfect place to rest for the day. If I wanted to rest. Which I didn't. I wanted to go home.

I turned to tell him we should keep going, but he tossed me over his shoulder before I could argue. Seething, I kept quiet as he sprinted toward the house. Behind us, the sky was just barely starting to lighten. In the daylight, I could maybe manage on my own.

The sudden jump he executed made my stomach drop. When he landed, I patted his back.

"Put me down."

He stopped moving and set me on my feet.

"This time you go inside first and check for infected."

He blinked at me, grunted, then went to the entrance. I watched him put his shoulder to the door. As soon as it gave way, he went inside.

I moved quickly to the fence and prepared to jump and catch the top. A whisper of movement on the other side stopped me. Leaning closer, I peeked through the tiny gap in the board and almost screamed at the sight of an infected looking straight at me. Slowly, I backed away and edged closer to the door and Drav.

Drav came out several moments later with a body and a head. I almost yipped at his sudden appearance.

"Inside, Mya," he said, after he dumped them over the fence.

I willingly turned from the fence—and what lurked beyond—and walked into the house with Drav right behind me. He went to the kitchen to start searching cupboards, and I noted the thick blood that spattered his shirt in several places. Tearing off heads was messy business.

"I need to pee," I said, watching him.

He grunted and moved toward the hall. I followed him. As soon as I found a bathroom, I stepped in, closed the curtains, and turned on the light.

"Door open," he said over his shoulder as he headed back to the kitchen.

Seeing the infected on the other side of the fence had killed any urge to leave. Still, I kept the door open as I quickly used the bathroom and washed my hands. By the time I returned to the kitchen, Drav already had several cans of food open. I ate some chili and green beans. He consumed three cans of tuna and tried a bite of peas, which he swallowed but obviously didn't like, given the way he shoved the can aside.

"Not good?" I asked, trying not to laugh.

"Not good," he said, agreeing.

Once we finished, I wandered off in search of a bedroom before he could start his nudging. In the first one I found, I went to the closet to look for a shirt that might fit him.

"Mya, no," he said, snagging me around the waist and turning me toward the bed.

"Drav, stop. Wait." He let me go, and I turned to point at the blood on his clothes.

"You can't sleep in that shirt. It has infected blood all over it, and it's gross." But more importantly...what if it got into his gash and he turned into one of them? I wouldn't stand a chance.

He grunted and had his shirt untied and off in two blinks. My brain malfunctioned slightly at the sight of all that chiseled, muscled flesh.

"Ohhh-kay. Ah, I'll just see if I can find you a new one."

He blocked my step toward the closet then slowly moved toward me. I retreated, until I realized he was backing me toward the bed. Thoughts of how he'd pressed against me yesterday while I slept and his current exposed state had me scrambling for a way to distract him. The red spotting his white bandage caught my eye.

"Wait. I, uh, should check that cut on your side." I gestured at it. "We should clean and change that."

"Yes," he said, stepping back.

Relieved, I hurried from the room to the bathroom, where I dug out what I could find for first aid supplies. There wasn't much. With a tube of ointment and several knee-sized band-aids on the counter, I faced Drav, who waited in the doorway.

He didn't make a sound as I eased the old bandage away. One part stuck and I had to carefully wet the cloth before removing it. After reapplying ointment, I put several new band-aids on. He waited in the hall while I threw away the wrappers and washed my hands.

"I'll get you a clean shirt," I said as I joined him.

"No clean shirt."

Crap. I didn't resist his nudge toward the bedroom as I struggled to think of another solution to my half-naked demon problem.

"There's another bedroom if you'd rather have a bed to yourself," I said.

"No. You go outside."

Damn. Unable to think of anything else to prevent snuggle time without making him angry, I reluctantly entered the room. Before I reached the bed, he tugged at the bottom of my shirt.

"Gross, Mya."

I turned to face him, understanding what he was saying.

Up to this point he had been relatively respectful when I asked him to give me a sliver of privacy, so I shook my head and took a step backwards.

Drav pulled at my shirt again.

"It has infected blood all over it," he said, using my words.

Glancing down, I saw flecks of spattered dark brown blood mixed in with the grunge from falling, sweating, and other mishaps on the road. Yeah, my shirt looked pretty gross, but I wasn't about to part with it, not with his fascination with my boobs.

"No, my shirt stays on."

"No shirt."

"Yes shirt."

Dear lord, now I was arguing like him. Before he could say anything, a jaw-cracking yawn took me by surprise. Drav stared at my wide-open mouth. The yawn ended with his finger lifting my upper lip.

"What the hell, Drav?" I said as he bent down to take a closer look.

Drav's lips parted as he slid his tongue down one of his long, sharp canines.

"Yeah, we have different size teeth," I said, pulling back. He dropped his inquisitive fingers and glanced at my top again.

"I will sleep easier with my shirt on."

I climbed into the bed, and Drav grunted, which I took to mean he would allow me to keep my shirt.

Once I settled in on my side with my back to him—the safest position, in my mind—he lay down behind me and wrapped an arm around my waist. His hand drifted dangerously close to the prize he'd held this morning. I frowned as I realized it hadn't been this morning because the sun was just rising. Traveling at night and sleeping during the day was messing with my head. How long had it been since the first attack? Two nights ago?

His hand crept closer, his fingers brushing my underwire, and I quickly grasped his wrist. The feel of something under my palm had me looking down. A leather bracelet wrapped around his wrist. I tried lifting his hand, but he didn't budge.

"No, Mya." Drav whispered, his breath warm against the back of my neck.

"I'm not leaving. I just want to look at your bracelet."

His tight hold on my waist loosened, and this time, he let me lift his arm. A beautifully crafted bracelet, leather bound with rough crystal with markings engraved on the top, circled his wrist. I touched the crystal, my finger tracing the marking.

Drav hummed and snuggled closer. Carefully, I set his arm back down where it had been. His chest expanded against my back as he drew in a deep breath.

"Sleep, Mya."

After running through Oklahoma City the whole night, my body felt like lead. Hoping I wasn't making a mistake, I closed my eyes.

*   *   *   *

I was blissfully warm and well-rested when I woke, too cozy to want to open my eyes. That changed the moment a warm hand stroked the bare skin of my back.

My eyes popped open, and I stared at the expanse of grey-honed skin before me. At some point in the night, I had turned in my sleep and now lay chest to chest with Drav. I looked up to find him watching me. His hand didn't still on my back as our gazes locked. Uncertain if a roving hand on my back was any safer than an over the shirt boob grab, I tried to scoot backwards, but he held me tight.

"No, Mya."

"I wish I hadn't taught you that word."

My stomach growled, which caught Drav's attention. He glanced down between us with a concerned frown.

"Just hungry," I said.

"Hungry, Mya."

I nodded, and he rolled away from me, sitting up. With some breathing room, I glanced at the windows and noticed the weak light peeking around the curtains. Another day gone and another night waited filled with running from things that wanted to kill me.

"Did you want to put your shirt back on?" I asked when I finally looked his way.

"No. Gross."

He held out his hand, but I ignored it and slipped out of bed on my own.

After I made a pit-stop at the bathroom, where Drav again insisted I keep the door open, we ate a quick meal of canned food. Drav watched me carefully through our "breakfast," and I avoided looking at him. His bare chest was intimidating.

Once we finished eating, we made our way back outside where the sun had dipped below the horizon.

Without any warning, he threw me over his shoulder and jumped the fence, giving me no chance to warn him about the infected I'd seen that morning. A second later, Drav landed and set me on my feet. I looked around with wide eyes. Thankfully, the infected person no longer waited on this side. I was so ready to be done with this trip home.

ELEVEN

Gathering my courage, I turned toward the side yard and made my way to the front. The streets were quiet as I slipped behind a camper parked in a driveway.

We took care moving from yard to yard, neighborhood to neighborhood. The quarter moon rose, and Drav moved confidently in its weak light, obviously having an easier time seeing now than he did in the daylight.

The roads became familiar as we moved closer to my neighborhood, and a quiet settling warmth filled me. *Home.* Yet, it would not be the home I remembered. The white bedsheets that flapped in the night breeze of a couple of homes we passed made that point clear. I hoped there were still people inside and that there would be a similar sign at my house.

I readied myself to make the next sprint when Drav halted me with a hand on my shoulder. Like last night, he'd kept me from running into any of the infected. He watched everything carefully, and if he spotted something I didn't, he nudged me in a different direction.

Now, I glanced at him while he alertly searched the streets.

"Drav?"

"Mya, stay."

He walked off, but didn't go too far before he stopped. It wasn't until I heard the quiet rustle of fabric and a spatter of liquid that I gathered he was relieving himself. I turned away, my cheeks still hot as I tried to give him as much privacy as possible. Had he been relieving himself outside all along? How had I not noticed?

Drav returned to my side, and I moved to the next area of cover, refusing to acknowledge that he'd just gone to the bathroom in the open street.

My anxiety grew the closer we got to my neighborhood because I had noticed a few houses that were lit up. A living person wouldn't want to draw attention to themselves; they would have turned off the lights. We crossed the road where my elementary best friend, Amber, lived. I didn't have the heart to glance at her house to see if there were any signs of life.

We crossed between two more houses with fences, where Drav lifted me over his shoulder and jumped, before we reached my street. Halfway down, the familiar sight of my house greeted me. Instead of rushing forward to the next tree, I hesitated. I couldn't shake the worry that once I got to my house, the lights would be on and there would be slow, unnatural movement in the windows or the windows would be dark with no signs of life, and Drav and I would go inside and he would rip off the heads of my family. I shuddered at the thought.

Drav put a hand on my shoulder again when I would have moved. I stayed by the tree while Drav disappeared for a moment. Instead of relieving himself, I heard the distinct snap and squelch I'd come to associate with his head ripping. I tried not to freak out. He didn't just kill a member of my family, did he? No, I had to stay positive that they were safe. Ryan's last text warned me about the hounds. That meant he'd known what was happening. The thought of his last text had me touching my back pocket to reassure myself my phone was still there.

Drav rejoined me, and I sprinted across the street, ducking behind a large SUV that belonged to our neighbors only two houses away. From my angle, I could see my house. The blinds were drawn, and the lights were off. Excitement, fear, and emotional exhaustion had my hands shaking.

I ran from my hiding spot, heading straight for my house. Before I could reach for the doorknob, my hand met unrelenting flesh. I looked up in surprise and found Drav frowning down at me.

"No, Mya."

"This is my home. My family is in there."

"No. Drav go."

"You can't," I said in panic. If he went in there, he might kill my family.

"No. They're fine, safe. I need to go in." I tried to step around him, but he blocked me.

"No."

"Yes, Drav."

In my desperation to get inside I forgot who I was dealing with and pushed on his chest to emphasize my point. I swallowed hard and backed up fearful of how he would react.

He didn't do much more than scowl at me, but he made his stance clear. He wouldn't let me in.

"What if we go in together?" I asked, attempting to compromise. "But you can't hurt anyone. Please."

He didn't look happy about it, but he could tell I wasn't going to budge.

"Yes?" I prompted.

"Yes."

He moved aside, and I set my hand on the knob. For a moment, I couldn't bring myself to turn it. I sucked in a breath and twisted. The door caught, locked of course.

"Drav, I need you to open the door, but just open it."

I moved out of his way. He grabbed hold of the doorknob, gave it a sharp turn, and put his shoulder to the door. The frame cracked, and the door swung inwards revealing an inky darkness.

Drav touched the edge of my shirt and coiled it in his hold. We entered together. I didn't hear anything, and I worried what that meant.

Fear bubbled up my chest. I couldn't hold it in anymore.

"Mom? Dad? Ryan?"

My brother's name came out as a hoarse cry, which Drav smothered with his hand. His low growl rose around us.

A sick dread twisted in my stomach as I held still and listened.

Please not my family, I thought.

A soft feline growl reached me, and a sob of relief escaped. I pushed Drav's hand from my mouth.

"Pots," I said softly. "Come here, kitty kitty."

The cat hissed in the darkness before us, and Drav growled in response.

"It's okay, Drav. It's our cat. A pet."

I tried to step forward but Drav blocked me. Instead of arguing, I stepped back, used the dead bolt to latch the door, and felt for the wall switch.

"I'm turning on the lights," I warned a moment before I did.

Drav grunted, and I squinted as I looked around the entry and dining room.

"No infected. Let's keep checking," I said with relief.

This time when I stepped forward, he moved with me.

Pots shot down the hall when we turned the corner and walked into the kitchen. I barely paid Drav's growl at my cat any attention because a note on the fridge had caught my eye.

I crossed the room and snatched the paper from the magnet.

> *Mya,*
>
> *We love you so much. We've seen the dogs and what they do. We're heading to the cabin and hope you're already there and never read this. But, if you do come home first, stay strong. Stay safe. Get out of town, and try to get to the cabin. We'll be waiting for you there. If you're not there in two days, we'll come find you.*
>
> *Love, Mom and Dad*

I sniffled past the tears and focused on the note Ryan had

scribbled below my parents' message.

> The dogs hate light. Travel during the day, and hide somewhere bright at night. Left you a present in my closet. Get your ass to the cabin. Love, Ryan.

They hadn't been infected. At least, not here. I wiped my eyes, folded the paper, and tucked it in my back pocket. My fingers brushed my phone and I pulled it out, checking it again. The low battery and no signal didn't give me any hope.

"Mya," Drav said from behind me. I turned and found his watery gaze on mine.

He, like the dogs, didn't like the light. And, since he didn't seem inclined to leave me that meant I'd be traveling in the dark. With the hounds. And the infected. And, according to Jack and Charles, the other shadow men.

"My family isn't here. They headed north." I glanced at a clock. We still had hours of night left. Plenty of time.

"I'm going to grab some things and then we can get moving again."

"No lights," he said, pointing toward the ceiling light.

"I can't see in the dark like you. And the infected aren't attracted to lights. They're attracted to noise. And the hounds are afraid of lights. I'm turning every light on in the house. Here," I said moving to the fridge. I plucked a pair of my Dad's sunglasses off the top. "Put these on and don't touch the lights or...or I'll throw the cat at you."

He frowned at me but took the glasses. I didn't wait to see if he'd use them.

Heading down the hall, I started thinking of what it would take to make it to the cabin. There wouldn't be as many houses to raid for supplies once we left city limits. So I'd need basic things. A water bottle. Simple food. Warmer clothes.

In Ryan's room, I checked the closet and found one of my dad's burns-your-retinas-like-the-sun flashlights on the shelf. Ryan's foresight had me grinning. If any family had a chance at surviving this mess, it would be ours because of Ryan. I reached under his bed hoping for his hiking bag, but found the space empty. Having the bag would have made my life easier but there were other options.

I turned around and almost face-planted into Drav's chest. The smooth skin of his pec brushed my nose before I backed up a step.

He looked down at me. Despite the tinted lenses of the sunglasses, I could still see his eyes watering a little bit.

"Can you see better? With the glasses on?"

"Yes. No."

"So, just a little better?"

"Yes. Mya go outside."

"Not yet. I need to grab some more stuff."

Going to my parents' room, I looked for the next thing that would make my life easier...something for Drav to wear now and several spares for later. His head ripping, while it kept me safe, was disgusting and messy.

Dad's robust figure meant the shirts had a decent amount of girth, but he didn't even come close to Drav's height. As I studied the selection I had to choose from, I wondered if any of them would even reach Drav's navel.

I tossed a few dark options on my parents' bed.

"Try those on. I'm going to grab some clean clothes for myself."

In my room, I stuffed an old backpack with two clean changes of clothes, the flashlight, and a sweatshirt. I shouldered the bag and turned to find Drav, still shirtless, standing in my room. His continued shirtlessness didn't surprise me. My reflection in the mirror just behind him did.

Dark spatters and splotches covered my face and shirt. Stepping closer to the mirror, I cringed at the dot that stuck to my skin dangerously close to my mouth. Infected blood. My stomach churned and a hint of panicked paranoia burrowed into my mind. What did it take to become infected? A bite from a hound, yes, but were there other ways? Obviously so, because it was spreading like crazy. Bites from the infected. Charles had said that, hadn't he? Bites were a form of fluid exchange...like ingesting a drop of blood. How close had I come to being infected without even knowing it?

A chill chased through me. I didn't want to touch the blood but I wanted it off. Now.

"Are we safe in here?" I asked.

"Yes."

"For how long?"

"Long."

"Ok. I'm going to clean up. This blood is giving me a mental twitch."

Without waiting for a response, I paced down the hall to the bathroom I shared with Ryan. I started closing the door and groaned when Drav stopped it with the flat of his hand.

"Mya, no."

"Drav, I'm not running away again. I promise. I'm cleaning the blood off me and changing my clothes. You don't need to see that. I'll be out when I'm done."

"Infected outside. Hounds outside."

"Yeah, I know. That's why I'm inside with all the lights on."

He studied me from behind his lenses before grunting and releasing his hold on the door. He even backed up a step. But he didn't walk away. I closed the door in his face and locked it.

"Mya," I heard through the door.

"Drav, stay out."

I pulled off my clothes, started the shower, and stepped in. I didn't care that the water still ran cold. I needed the blood off me.

Before I'd wet more than my shins, the door splintered and a bang filled the room. A startled scream escaped me, followed by another when the curtain and rod were completely ripped from the wall.

TWELVE

Drav and I stared at each other. For a moment, I'd thought an infected had broken in, and relief swelled at the sight of him before anger overwhelmed it. What the hell had he barged in for? His gaze remained locked on my very exposed breasts then moved lower. Fear of Drav began to worm its way back into my mind.

I slapped one arm across my chest and used the other to shield my lady bits. It didn't stop him from staring.

"Drav, leave."

"No."

He tilted his head, continuing his perusal, and frowned. My panic started to rise.

"Boobs," he said, pointing at my chest. Then he pointed at his own. "No boobs." Next, he grabbed at his happy stick with one hand and reached for my crotch with the other.

I pressed back against the tile and swatted his hand away.

"Yeah. Congratulations. You've noticed I have no penis. Most girls don't. Now stop staring and give me back the shower curtain so I can finish washing."

He bent down and reached for the fallen curtain and rod, but his gaze zeroed in on my crotch once more. He forgot about the curtain and leaned forward.

"Back off Drav or I'm going to kick you in the damn face. This isn't anatomy class." Fear shuddered through me.

"No penis. See better?"

"Hell no!"

He grunted and straightened. Then he focused on the now steaming water and the shower head. He raised his hand and put his fingers in the water. He sniffed them and grunted again.

My heart thundered in my chest as I watched him reach for the string holding his pants up.

"Stop." The word came out breathless in my growing panic.

He froze and blinked at me, an action I began to suspect he did when he didn't understand something. Figuring I had little to lose by stating the truth, I started talking.

"I'm terrified. Of the infected. Of the hounds. Of you. Of why you didn't kill me. I can't keep going like this. I just wanted to go home to know my family was safe. But my family isn't here. I want my family. I want to be safe."

He tilted his head at me.

"I didn't kill you. Boobs. No penis."

"You didn't kill me because I'm a girl?"

"Yes."

I swallowed hard and blinked against the sudden sting in my eyes. Would he now start doing more than looking and groping?

"What are you going to do?" My voice warbled.

He blinked back at me. "Keep you safe. Take you home."

Too afraid to hope and too afraid to be anything but more

afraid, I sniffled.

"Mya, clean."

"I can't with you watching me," I said, desperate for him to leave and let me just think for a minute.

"Why?" he asked.

"Because it makes me uncomfortable."

He bent down and picked up the shower curtain and rod and handed it to me. Sacrificing my cover, I reached for it. He pulled back a little bit, his gaze inspecting my bits again.

"Please just let me have the shower curtain."

He grunted and gave it over. I quickly put the tension rod back in place, knowing Drav wasn't leaving.

"No touching the curtain," I said, staring at the white material blocking me from his view.

"Clean, Mya." He said it like an order.

"Fine." I exhaled shakily and stepped into the spray.

Paranoia still held me in its grip. I felt certain I would somehow become infected. So I kept my eyes and mouth closed as I soaped and rinsed. Then I began to worry that Drav might try to watch me while my eyes were closed. Because of that, I took the fastest shower of my life.

When I turned off the water, Drav spoke up from the other side of the curtain.

"Mya, no. Let me shower."

His increasing spurts of sensible speech continued to surprise me. Who learned that fast?

"I'll turn the shower back on for you. But, you need to leave now so I can get a towel and dry off."

I waited behind the curtain, listening. The door opened

followed by a soft sound that I thought might be it closing. It was hard to tell since I didn't know in what condition he'd left the door. I hadn't even thought to look at the damage after he'd ripped away the shower curtain.

I hesitated a few moments, then hearing nothing, I peeked out.

Drav stood by the bathroom closet with a hand towel in one hand and a folded bath towel in the other. When he heard the curtain, he turned toward me and held both up.

The pieces of material in his hands barely registered as I stared at his now very naked bottom half.

"Towel?" he asked.

I couldn't help but look. Yes, he'd waved his goods around when we'd first met, but I'd been scared beyond imagination. I still felt jumpy and freaked out, but I also started to believe him. He acted like he'd never seen a girl before. He'd killed any infected or hound that came near me for the past two days, and he'd admitted he wanted to keep me safe. On top of all of that, he did help me get home.

His eyes still seemed weird to me. Also, the ease in which he killed really worried me. And, his semi-erection didn't ease my fears about what might yet happen if I continued in his company. But, for now, it seemed like I'd gotten my wish. I was safe.

"Yeah, those are towels. We use the bigger ones to dry our bodies. The smaller one is for drying our hands when we wash them in the sink."

He grunted and brought the bigger towel to me. Keeping the curtain between us, I reached for it. This time, he didn't tease me by keeping it out of my reach.

With the towel in hand, I ducked back behind the curtain and quickly dried off. The big towel adequately covered my torso so I could step out without exposing myself.

Drav hadn't moved, which made my exit a little cozy. He took the opportunity to lean in to sniff me.

"Why do you do that? Smell me, I mean. Do I smell bad? Good? Please don't say you think of chicken when you smell me."

"You smell good. Not Drav." He didn't lean back to speak, so his words, close to my ear, made me shiver.

"I smell different than you?" I asked, trying to ignore how very uncomfortable he was making me.

"Yes."

"It's probably the soap," I said.

I turned my back to him, pulled open the curtain, and reached for one of the bottles on the shower caddy. Drav's hand slid up along my leg.

"Hey," I said, quickly spinning around holding the bottle. "No touching."

"Why no touching?"

"Because it makes me uncomfortable."

"What not makes Mya uncomfortable?"

"At this point in my life, everything is making me uncomfortable," I said, giving him a flat look.

"Towel uncomfortable?" The sly way he said it, and the slight upward curve on his mouth, made me snort.

"Nice try, buddy. The towel is staying on, and you're keeping your hands to yourself. Now, do you want me to explain how to use this stuff or not."

"Explain."

I quickly went over turning the water on and off and how to wash and rinse—along with a caution not to let soap get in his eyes—and suggested he remove his bandages.

"Mya clean it."

"Nope, not this time. The shower will clean it."

He grunted then tore off the bandages without a wince. The wound already appeared well on its way to being healed.

Lacking any hint of modesty, he lifted his leg high and stepped into the shower. Swallowing hard at the well-endowed sight of him, I turned away to grab my bag and leave the bathroom. The sound of the curtain closing and the shower starting assured me that he now believed I wouldn't run. And, I wouldn't. A considerable number of zombie infested miles still separated me from the cabin. I had the smarts to know that sticking with Drav increased my chances of seeing my family alive.

Holding the towel tightly around my body, I made my way down the hall to my room. Even with all the lights on, the house felt eerie in its silence. Usually, Ryan had music playing or a TV show on, and the washer or drier would be running non-stop. I couldn't help but smile a little at the memory. It always amazed Mom how much laundry four people could produce.

In my room, I hurried to dig through my drawers for fresh clothes. Although Drav had set aside his curiosity about our physical differences just now, I knew it would resurface if he finished his shower before I managed to dress. Dropping the towel, I put on fresh underwear and a clean bra. It almost made me feel human again.

I tugged on a pair of jeans and a tank-top before digging in my closet for an old hoodie. Walking here had been chilly, and it would only grow more so as the days passed. The hoodie I found had enough substance to it to keep me warm. I put it on, glad to get the mass of wet hair off my back.

After towel drying my hair, I searched the top of my dresser for a hair-tie. I scraped my fingers through the wet strands and wrapped my long, thick hair into a tight bun on the back of my head.

Glancing around the room, I tried to decide what more I needed in my bag. The thought of the blood splatter so close to my lips made me shudder. Soaps and washcloths were a must.

"Mya," Drav bellowed.

I poked my head into the hallway. Drav stood just outside the bathroom door, dripping wet from his shower. His long black hair, the only thing covering him, hung loosely over his chest almost to his bellybutton.

When he saw me, rage lit his eyes. He stormed toward me while stringing together a bunch of words and noises I couldn't understand.

"Whoa, what? Drav, what's wrong?"

He clutched his hair, then touched my head. I frowned, confused and just a bit afraid.

"You don't like my hair up? You had yours up."

"Where hair, Mya?"

He was having a fit over my hair?

"I tied it back."

His hand gripped my shoulder, and he spun me around. I felt a tug on my bun. A moment later, my wet hair came tumbling down. He combed his fingers through the strands and pulled them away from my neck. A glance back confirmed he was once again smelling my hair. A contented rumble sounded from his chest.

Okay, time to stop whatever was happening.

"Please let go of my hair and go put some pants on. You're making me uncomfortable."

Drav let out a quiet growl, clearly agitated that I stopped him mid-sniff, but he released my hair and left the room. I exhaled slowly, releasing any lingering anxiety. The things that set him off would probably never make sense to me.

Focusing on my bag, I considered what we would need. It all depended on how long we'd be gone and how we'd be traveling. The cabin was a little over an hour away, roughly, by car. However, taking a vehicle seemed out of the question, given what Drav had done to the truck. Plus, the noise of the engine would draw too much attention from the infected. That left walking, which would take forever, especially since Drav would only allow us to walk at night. I tried doing the math in my head, using a five mile an hour estimate, and guessed it would take at least three nights of walking, minimum. More if we ran into trouble. So, I needed to pack light. I couldn't be weighed down if I needed to run.

I added three more pair of underwear and socks to what I already had packed, then left my bag on my bed while I went to my parents' room to see what would fit Drav. He joined me a moment later. This time with pants on.

"Go ahead and try those shirts on," I said, pointing to the shirts I'd laid out on the bed. I turned back to the closet to start searching for more options.

Behind me I heard the sound of fabric rustling, and I glanced at Drav in the mirror.

Drav tried to pull the first t-shirt over his head, but the material got stuck by his ears. I hurried to him and helped tug the shirt the rest of the way down. It circled his neck snuggly, but he didn't seem to notice. Instead, he continued to attempt squeezing into what I'd given him. A stitch ripped.

"Hold up. You can ditch that one."

I started to help yank the tight fabric over his head, but he wrapped his hands around the neckline and ripped the top down the middle. I stared at the two pieces. He'd just ripped the shirt I had given my dad after I finished my freshman year at OU.

"Oooh-kay, try this one." I handed him an oversized flannel shirt.

Drav manage to tug the shirt on, but the sleeves were tight around the biceps. One good flex and he'd be sleeveless.

"Hang on. Let me go grab some of my brother's stuff." Ryan took after our dad but often bought a size too big to use when working out.

I rifled through Ryan's things, looking for his workout clothes. The athletic shorts would probably work if Drav needed something beside his sturdy pants. I tugged out a couple of longer navy t-shirts and a pair of loose black shorts.

With my new finds bundled in my arms, I went to my

room for scissors so I could cut into the neckline. Drav walked in before I finished.

"Got more shirts for you to try."

I held up one of the t-shirts. He pulled it over his head. While the neckline was looser, thanks to the cut I'd made, the rest of the shirt molded to him like a second skin once he got his arms through the sleeves.

"A bit snug but it will do. Let's find a bag and we can head out."

"Head out?"

"We have to go to my grandfather's cabin. North of here."

I tucked his extra clothes into the bag with my stuff then went to the bathroom for the washcloth and soap. I was very tempted to take the toilet paper, just in case, but knew I didn't have much room left. Two travel packs of tissues were the next best thing.

Drav watched me from the doorway as I set everything on the bathroom counter and opened a vanity drawer. Before looking in my bedroom mirror, I hadn't realized how disgusting I'd gotten. Now that I knew what to expect while traveling with Drav, I pulled three bands from my stash of hair ties.

I raked my fingers through my hair to throw it up in a messy bun. Drav grabbed my wrist gently and stopped the movements.

"Come." He nudged me out of the bathroom back to my room where he tried steering me to the bed.

"No, Drav. We still have plenty of night left. We have to go, not sleep." Finding my family already gone had been a huge disappointment. The longer we stayed, the longer it would take us to find them, and the less chance I had of finding them healthy.

When I turned to go back to the bathroom, he picked me up and sat me down on the bed. I glared up at him.

"Stay. Mya hair." He tugged at his strands then gently did the same to mine.

"Are you telling me I can't go outside with a wet head? Because, that's dumb."

"No. Mya hair. Stay."

He sat beside me and combed his fingers through my hair.

"We don't have time for this," I said, growing frustrated with his apparent hair fetish.

I moved to stand, but his hand caught my thigh and I sat back down with an "oof."

"Hair," he said, sharply.

He leaned in to smell it again, but before I could complain some more, his fingers delved into my hair. With quick, sure movements, he created three sections, gently parting the strands. I sighed and resigned myself to allowing him to play with my hair for a few minutes, hoping it would be enough time to get it out of his system.

A couple of times, he found knots, which he slowly worked through. I focused on the mirror on the other side of the room and watched as he fashioned three French braids, two on the sides and one on the top of my head. When he finished, I had three braids tied together in the back. I looked stunningly badass, and his skill at braiding amazed me. The hair style would keep my hair much cleaner.

I twisted on the bed and patted his knee.

"Thank you."

I left before he could respond.

In the bathroom, I grabbed the items I had planned to take. From there, I went to the kitchen and filled two reusable water bottles. I was checking the cabinets for light-weight portable food when Drav joined me. He'd braided his hair much like mine.

"Are you hungry?" I asked.

"Are you?"

"I suppose we should eat before we head out."

I pulled out a can of pineapple chunks, popped the top open, and set it in front of Drav before turning back to the cupboards. We had a ton of canned food, but that would be too heavy.

"Mya."

"Hmm."

Drav captured me by the shoulders and led me back to the table.

"Mya, hungry. Eat."

He didn't give me much of a choice. Sitting, I stuffed a chunk of pineapple in my mouth then attempted to stand again. He pushed me back into my seat and tried to feed me another piece. He didn't relent and started to growl in frustration when I kept trying to get up and pack. I eventually gave in and ate the food he offered.

Once we finished with our small meal, he helped me pack some granola bars and trail mix. I lifted my bag, judging the weight of it. Manageable. Sliding it onto my back, I looked around the kitchen one last time.

The waning moon, still high in the sky, confirmed we had plenty of night remaining. But, leaving proved harder than I'd thought. A quiet part of my mind, because I had refused to acknowledge it, reared its ugly head.

What if this was the last time I saw home?

I shook my head. My family was my home, not the house or objects inside of it. None of that stuff mattered. Well, besides our cat. However, considering his reaction to Drav, he couldn't come with us. I placed his bag of food out on the floor with the top open. He would have to self-feed, but I knew he would be okay until we could come back and get him.

Drav went outside first and beckoned me forward. I set the direction, heading northwest toward my family's cabin.

THIRTEEN

Once we left the last of the city lights and infected behind us, Drav walked beside me. We didn't talk. Noise carried too far in the dark. Even the soft brush of our passing through the dried grass worried me. However, Drav didn't seem as tense now that we'd abandoned the city. He walked with fluid ease, taking slower steps so I didn't have to jog to keep up as we traveled the countryside.

Before the hellhounds invaded, we would have seen headlights on the roads we crossed or heard the distant hum of engines on the highway we passed. Instead, there was silence. Not even the chirp of crickets or chatter of small animals could be heard. The silence was the one unsettling, continuous reminder of just how much the world had changed. So, I focused on the slight sound of our passing until something distracted me.

In the trees to our right, I saw a dot of light. White, not red. It disappeared, but I kept my eye on the spot and saw the light again a few feet later. A distant yard light to a house nestled in the trees. I wondered if the people who lived there had escaped the notice of the hounds and the infected. I hoped so. If they could survive this close to the city, my family had an even better chance at our cabin.

Drav grabbed my arm without warning, jerking me to a stop. The aggressive way he angled himself in front of me and growled had my pulse spiking. I froze and peered ahead, trying to see what had provoked him. However, beyond the shadowy shapes of trees, shrubs, and grass, I couldn't see a damn thing. I moved closer to Drav and wished for my flashlight. I should have walked with it in my hand instead of stuffing it in my bag.

Drav growled again. From the darkness came a faint, answering growl. Something was definitely out there.

Slowly, Drav straightened and said something. It wasn't English, just a bunch of garbled nonsense to me. However, the same sounds came back from the dark. Another shadow man.

"Crap."

Drav loosened his hold on my arm and looked at me. Gently, he ran his fingers over the area he'd grabbed.

"I'm sorry, Mya. Arm fall off?" he questioned quietly.

I almost told him it wouldn't but reconsidered as I thought of the easy strength he'd used to pull the heads from all the infected bodies.

"Not yet. Who's out there?" I asked, looking into the darkness again.

A distance ahead of us, a shadow moved, steadily growing bigger. Big like Drav, confirming my suspicion.

"Is he going to want to kill me?" I asked, unable to stop myself.

"No."

Drav looked away from me and spoke to the approaching figure. I heard my name thrown in with the gibberish. When

Drav quieted, the shadow answered in a growly voice. Drav listened then looked down at me.

"Ghua good. Ghua family."

Ghua? Based on the tone of their conversation, I didn't feel reassured.

The new shadow man had finally walked close enough that I could see the subtle differences between the two men. While the dark loose shirt and pants seemed similar in style and color to what Drav had worn when I'd first met him, this shadow man's skin shone even darker than Drav's, almost black. The same reptilian like eyes blinked at me. However, Ghua's seemed more yellow than green and much creepier because of the coloring. His long black hair hung in a single braid that didn't quite match Drav's in length but still extended well past his shoulders.

Ghua said something more then started to crouch. Drav laughed, a first. The deep, soft sound unnerved me.

"What's going on?" I asked quietly.

"Mya, stay," Drav said, taking my shoulder and guiding me back a step. He let go and turned back to Ghua, whose white teeth flashed in the dark as he grinned. Drav crouched low and tensed. My stomach dipped and twisted sickeningly as I grasped what was about to happen.

They flew at each other. The impact made a deep thud in the dark. A growl escaped one of them as they grappled. Seeing the way Drav's muscles bulged in effort made me swallow hard. In all the head ripping he'd done, he'd never exerted himself the way he did now. Just how strong was he?

I had my answer when he laughed and flipped Ghua over

his back. Ghua landed with a thump. Drav reached out with one hand and picked him up by the neck. Ghua punched Drav in the ribs, drawing a pained grunt from him. Drav didn't let go, though. With his other hand, Drav gripped the top of Ghua's head in a familiar move.

"Drav, no," I said, far too loudly for my own comfort.

Drav paused, and Ghua stopped trying to hit Drav to look at me.

"I thought he was your family. Family don't kill each other."

Drav grunted, let go of Ghua, and said something I didn't understand. Ghua laughed in return.

Drav started talking again, and Ghua stared at me the entire time, his gaze shifting from my face to my hair then back to my face. His barely discernable brows started to sink lower on his forehead the longer Drav spoke. I didn't like not knowing what they were saying, but I wasn't kept wondering for long. Drav said a familiar word, and Ghua's gaze dropped to my chest.

Ghua made a noise of disbelief and tore his gaze from me to stare at Drav. When Ghua spoke, the tone seemed rough and demanding.

Drav began speaking once more and gestured with his hands near his chest. When he said "boobs," I cringed but kept quiet. My difference had kept Drav from killing me. If being an oddity kept me safer with Ghua, too, then Drav could explain away.

Ghua said something and they stopped talking. Both turned to look at me.

"Ghua want Mya to show boobs."

I crossed my arms over my chest.

"I am not showing my boobs to anyone, Drav. I told you, it makes me uncomfortable."

"Yes," Drav said before speaking to Ghua.

Ghua listened quietly until Drav gestured between his legs. Ghua made a choked sound, grabbed at his package, and spoke a few syllables. Drav grunted acknowledgment, and my cheeks turned red when Ghua's attention whipped to me. His gaze swept my face, then my chest, and finally he ducked his head a little as he tried his best to see through my pants.

Even clothed with jeans and a hoodie, I felt completely naked and exposed to his inquisitive gaze.

"Yep. No penis," I said.

Ghua started talking fast to Drav, who started talking just as fast back. Both fell completely silent again. Then, Ghua moved toward me.

"Ah...what's he doing?" I stepped behind Drav and kept him between me and Ghua when Ghua tried to follow.

"Mya, Ghua smell you."

"I don't want to be smelled. You've smelled me enough for both of you."

Drav caught me in his arms and pulled me to his chest. I struggled to push away from him, but he held firm.

"Drav, let me go." My words were muffled but still clear. He didn't release me, though.

Something brushed against my back. My face pressed into Dad's old shirt, I listened to Ghua get a good whiff of my hair. Anger boiled inside me. Drav held me still so his friend, who'd just wanted to see my boobs, could smell me. Hell no. I opened my mouth and bit Drav's chest. He grunted and abruptly released me. I surged back and solidly collided with Ghua. His arms came around me, and his hands landed just above my boobs.

Eyes wide, my mouth dropped open as his hands drifted lower and he thoroughly groped me.

Before I could yell, Drav stopped rubbing where I'd bitten him and growled. For a heartbeat, I thought he meant the growl for me. But when Ghua immediately let go, and Drav silently opened his arms for me without looking away from Ghua, I launched myself at Drav. He caught me, and his hand gently settled on the back of my head as he held me close.

He spoke to Ghua briefly in their language. When they quieted, I lifted my head enough to look up at Drav. He stared down at me in his unblinking way.

"Don't ever do that again. I'm not a toy. You don't get to share me."

"I won't share you. Ever," he said.

Not quite the reassurance I'd wanted. The way his hold had tightened on me just a smidge when he'd spoken didn't reassure me either. I eased myself from his arms and put some distance between us. He looked me over before focusing on Ghua, who watched us closely.

I studied the darkness around us while they started yet another quiet conversation. Not only were we wasting precious travel time, we weren't being quiet.

"Is it smart to be out in the open talking like this?" I asked, interrupting them. "How well do your hellhounds hear? I really don't want to get bitten by one."

Drav grunted and Ghua spoke briefly, gesturing back the way he'd come. Drav turned to me.

"Ghua go home with me and you. Keep Mya safe."

I didn't want Ghua traveling with us. He was still trying to see through my hoodie and my pants. But, standing in one place served no purpose.

"Fine. But no touching me."

"Yes," Drav said. Ghua answered with a clear, "yes" as well before he turned and headed back the way he'd just come.

Drav nudged me to follow.

"How are you learning my language so quickly?" I asked, walking.

Drav tapped his pointed ear.

"Just by listening?" I said.

"Yes."

"That's crazy."

Since Ghua was leading us, I moved closer to Drav.

"Do we have to stay with him? He's giving me the creeps with all his staring."

Ahead of us, Ghua grunted, which made me worry.

"Does he understand me?" I whispered to Drav.

"Yes."

After that, I kept quiet.

We didn't walk very far before Ghua veered into the trees. I kept close to Drav and tried to walk and breathe as quietly as possible while what little light the quarter moon provided faded even further under the barren branches.

When we stepped into a clearing with a house, Ghua headed straight for it. I tugged on Drav's arm.

"I don't want to go in there."

"Mya not stay outside."

The familiar phrase he used to get me inside for the day worried me.

"We're done walking for the night?"

"Yes."

"But why? We have hours of dark left yet."

"Drav listen to Ghua for the night."

I frowned trying to understand what he meant by that.

"He's your boss for tonight or you want to talk to him tonight?"

"I want to talk to Ghua tonight. We're walking"—he said something I didn't know—"night."

"Tonight we're going to talk with Ghua and tomorrow night we're walking again?" I guessed, hopefully.

"Yes."

"Without Ghua tomorrow night?"

"Yes."

"Fine. But no killing anyone in that house unless they're infected."

Drav grunted and spoke to Ghua who waited several yards away. Ghua answered then started toward the already broken in front door, and I realized whoever had been in there was probably already dead.

Following Drav into the house, I stepped into a neat and cozy living room. Drav closed the door behind me and started talking to Ghua. Unwilling to stand there and listen to a meaningless exchange, I went to the couch, turned on the lamp next to it, and sank into the comfy cushions with a sigh. Having a moment to just relax seemed surreal, and I soaked it up. Who knew what would happen from one moment to the next in this new world. I needed to start taking what I could get.

When the conversation stopped, I glanced at the pair and found them watching me.

"What? Am I not supposed to sit? We're staying the rest of the night, right?"

"Yes," Drav said, walking toward me. He looked at the couch then sat beside me. He studied the cushions a moment before running a hand over them.

"Comfy, isn't it?" I said.

"Yes."

Ghua went to a chair and sat as well.

Staying here with Ghua made me anxious. He still seemed too interested in the fact that I had boobs and no penis. Ignoring Ghua's stare, I turned to Drav.

"So what is he to you? Your brother? Cousin? Uncle?"

"No."

"Dad? Grandpa?" Ghua didn't look old enough to be either. "Nephew?"

"No."

"Oh, come on. I don't think I missed any...unless he's some kind of in-law."

"No."

"You're annoying me," I said, with a flat stare.

"Ghua is family, but not family."

"He's a friend?"

"Yes," Drav said happily.

I made a sound of disbelief. But, I didn't say anything more. Soon the two of them started talking, mixing English with their words. The more Drav said, the more Ghua started to say.

"Hold up," I said, interrupting them. "Do you really only need to hear a word once to understand it?"

"Yes," Drav said.

"Holy shit."

Fourteen

I tried to wrap my head around the concept of instant learning while the two of them continued their conversation. It made sense why Drav spoke such limited and broken English since I was the only one talking to him. Fear of being discovered by something that seemed to want to kill all humans had kept me from saying a lot.

Quietly, I considered the implications of their ability. That Drav could understand when I explained something could work in my favor.

Since their conversation contained only a few words of English, I lost interest in it and decided to go search for food. They stopped talking as soon as I walked into the hallway. Knowing Drav's concern, I peeked my head back into the room.

"Just going to the kitchen to find food."

Ghua's yellow eyes watched me intently, making my skin crawl. Drav grunted, pulling my attention to him. He stood and came toward me, which didn't bother me until Ghua stood as well.

"You can stay in there and talk."

"No, go to kitchen with Mya," Drav said, slipping past me to head down the hallway. I followed, not wanting to be left alone with Ghua.

The kitchen looked as if the world hadn't been upturned. Cozy and clean, it seemed like a place where someone's grandma had baked countless cookies.

Drav opened a cupboard door, and Ghua watched him while I continued to look around. My eyes caught on a dirty plate beside the sink. I stepped closer and saw one side of the double sink half filled with water. Clean dishes occupied the drying rack on the other side of the sink. A towel draped over one plate like it had just been set down. I couldn't look away from it.

"Were there people here?" I asked without looking at Ghua.

He spoke in his language, and Drav answered.

"There were infected outside."

I sighed and rubbed my face. It didn't mean anything that the people here hadn't escaped infection. They were close to the city. In the more rural locations, like our cabin, there would be less risk. My family would be fine.

Determined not to worry about what I couldn't control, I went to the pantry door as Drav searched in the cupboards. The closet was much bigger than I expected, and I tugged the string for the light in order to see.

There were cans of fruits on one shelf, boxed food on another, jugs of water and vinegar and jars of homemade jelly and pickles on another. The selection made my mouth water. Since Drav enjoyed the peaches and pineapples we had before, I grabbed those then stared longingly at a box of mac and cheese. It hadn't been that long ago since I had a hot meal, but it felt like years. If we were staying the night, I didn't see why I couldn't eat more than canned fruit. I snagged the box and came out.

Ghua stood with his back against the fridge, arms crossed. He and Drav were speaking again but more quietly this time.

"Do you guys want to try some mac and cheese?"

They stopped their talking and glanced at me.

"Never mind." I'd make it and if they wanted some, I'd share.

Setting the fruit and the box on the table, I turned toward the fridge.

"Excuse me. I need to get in there," I said, pointing at it.

Ghua moved to the side, and I stepped forward and pulled the door open. The homeowners might have had a stocked pantry, but the items in the fridge were on the light side. The half-gallon container of milk and the half sticks of butter made me think again of someone's grandma alone during that first night the hellhounds had appeared. Anger welled up inside of me. Why had this happened? I glanced at Drav, wanting to ask questions. Could I trust him to be honest? I just didn't know. Yes, he'd kept me safe. But, he admitted he'd only spared me because of my gender. What if my questions made him mad? Would his consideration for my gender go out the window?

"Mya?" Drav asked.

I realized I was just standing in front of an open fridge, staring at nothing, so I grabbed the milk and butter then turned around.

"You guys might as well sit," I said with a gesture at the table. "This will take a while."

While I searched for a pot, the guys took seats around the table. They continued to speak softly and I tried to listen to see if I could learn anything more about why they were here. However, I really couldn't understand much of what they said.

Filling the pot with water distracted me with a more pressing need. I had to pee. Ignoring it, I brought the pot to the stove and switched on the burner. However, the urge didn't go away. But, I didn't want the two of them hovering outside the bathroom door.

In an attempt to sneak out of the kitchen, I roamed the room until I reached the opening to the hallway.

"Mya, no."

Of course Drav had noticed.

"Just going to the bathroom. Can you keep an eye on the stove?"

Drav didn't say anything else so I swiftly retreated.

I found a half-bath tucked under the stairs leading to the second floor and quickly stepped in and shut the door. Unbuttoning my pants, I sat on the toilet placed under the sloped part of the ceiling.

I was finishing up when the doorknob twisted.

"Drav, I'm still in here."

It didn't stop him. The door swung open before I had my pants all the way up. Instead of Drav, Ghua stood in the doorway, watching with rapt interest as I finished yanking up my jeans. My cheeks flushed with embarrassment and anger.

Where the hell was Drav?

"Ghua." Drav's voice came from the hall as if my thoughts had brought him.

M.J. Haag and Becca Vincenza

Ghua flinched as Drav's lighter gray hand landed heavily on his shoulder with a loud clap. Ghua was pulled backward out of the doorway and replaced by Drav. His gaze swept over me from my head to my toes, and I hurriedly buttoned my jeans, grateful that my underwear had at least been up before Ghua had barged in.

Drav reached out and touched my cheek where I could feel the heated stain of embarrassment the strongest. His gaze held mine as his fingers smoothed over the spot. Abruptly, he turned and left me staring at an empty doorway.

Shakily exhaling, I went to wash my hands, but a thump of flesh meeting flesh in the hall interrupted me. Wiping my clean hands on my jeans, I cautiously peeked out the door.

Drav and Ghua stood near the base of the stairs. Ghua reached up and touched the blood dripping from his nose. He looked at his wet fingers then at Drav, who threw another punch. Ghua grinned, his smile bloody and his eyes sparkling with delight.

Drav drew back for another punch that Ghua didn't even try to block. Ghua's head snapped back, but he still didn't retaliate. He just stood there happily letting blood drip onto the floor while Drav beat him.

What was wrong with these two?

Drav took a step back just then.

"Friend," Ghua said.

Drav nodded and stuck his arm out. Ghua clasped Drav's forearm tightly, pulled him in for a quick hug, and released him with a shove.

Seriously? We had to stop walking for this?

Ignoring the pair, I stalked back to the kitchen and poured the noodles into the now boiling water. I felt a stab of betrayal that Drav had already forgiven Ghua for coming into the bathroom to sneak a peek. How ridiculous. Drav had done the same thing to me when we'd met. In fact, he had been much more forward than Ghua. I shook my head and stirred the noodles.

A chair scraped against the floor behind me, and I glanced over my shoulder to see the two of them in the kitchen. Ghua sat at the table, and Drav moved near me.

Ghua's eyes met mine, and his lips peeled back into a sharp toothed grin. I wished he would just go away. Glancing at the clock, I noted the time and turned back to the pot. I watched the pasta boil and let my mind wander as the two conversed in their language.

For the next eight minutes, I considered what was happening to the world outside this old house. What had caused the hellhounds and shadow men to appear? The obvious answer was the earthquakes. But why and how had the earthquakes brought them? The mysteries of our world were still being solved every day. But usually only small discoveries. How had we missed an entire species of intelligent beings? I glanced at Drav and considered the possibility that he was an alien.

The water started to boil over, distracting me from my thoughts. I turned down the heat and spooned a noodle out to test it, carefully blowing on the steamy shell before lifting it to my lips. It was still a little too firm when I bit down.

Ghua's chair clattered to the tiled floor as he stood with a growl. I jumped, startled, and turned to stare at him with wide eyes. He spoke sharply to Drav, gesturing at me, then left the room. I glanced at Drav. He stared at the empty hallway. While I didn't mind Ghua leaving, how he left made me nervous.

"Is something wrong?" I asked.

Drav studied me for a moment.

"No. You stay."

He left the kitchen, presumably to talk to Ghua, and I dug out a strainer for the noodles. By the time I finished up the mac and cheese, both men had returned to the kitchen. I set out three plates and spooned equal portions to each plate.

After opening a can of mandarin oranges, I drained the juice and found a bowl to put them in. Both men watched me set the bowl in the middle of the table, but neither reached for the food even after I sat.

I glanced at Ghua, who looked annoyed. Did they think I'd poisoned it or something? Picking up my spoon, I scooped up some noodles. Drav watched with interest but made no move to eat. Ghua watched Drav, his eyes narrowing a fraction. I shoved the hot noodles in my mouth and wanted to sigh happily. It was, by far, not the most elegant meal, but it reminded me of home. Of happier times, eating and sharing with Ryan. Or rather, fighting with Ryan to get the last bit.

"Eat," I said, feeling uncomfortable with their hesitation.

Drav gripped the spoon, scooped some up, and carefully lifted the bite to his lips. I watched as he chewed slowly then with more enthusiasm. After he swallowed, he went for another bite. I followed suit.

Ghua ignored the spoon and scooped his cheesy noodles up with his fingers. He didn't look bothered by the heat and ate with gusto. Whatever had upset Ghua seemed to no longer be a problem. Eventually, Drav gave up on the spoon, too, eating faster without it.

When they cleared their plates, both looked at me expectantly.

"It's all gone. Sorry, guys. Try the oranges."

We finished our meal, and they started talking, mostly in their language. I set the plates on top of the other dirty plate beside the sink and considered washing them. The world was going to shit, and the owner would never return. Who cared about clean dishes? Yet, as I looked at the neatly folded towel, I couldn't walk away. I emptied the sink of the cold water and quickly cleaned up the mess we'd made. When everything was back to the way we'd found it, I left the kitchen for the living room.

The couch called to me, and I cuddled up. The murmur of their voices lulled me, and full from the warm meal, it didn't take long for me to sleep.

A jostle to my arm woke me. I groaned and opened my eyes to find Drav bent over me like he was getting ready to pick me up.

"I can walk," I said.

He didn't move away.

"Back off, I can't get up."

He grunted and took a step back. Once I stood, he led me through the house to one of the bedrooms with a neatly made queen-sized bed. It looked very inviting. Tired and ready to go right back to sleep, I headed for the bed, but Drav stopped me with a tug at my shirt.

It took a moment to understand why. When I did, I pulled my shirt out of his hand.

"Nope. It's staying on. It's not dirty."

Drav huffed but let me climb into bed with my shirt on. He took his off, however, and snatched me around the waist when he joined me.

I fell back to sleep within seconds.

Fifteen

Sweat coated my neck and chest. Not a pleasant sensation to wake to. Drav held me closely, one hand under my shirt, fingers spread so his thumb rested just under my bra line and the tip of his pinky touched the waist of my low riding jeans. The position felt entirely too comfortable despite the sweat.

I grabbed his hand and untangled it from under my clothes. He pressed closer to me, his breath tickling my ear.

"Mya, no," he said, trying to put his hand back.

"Drav, no. You don't get to touch me whenever you want. It's rude. I thought we talked about that."

He sighed and rolled away. Cool air brushed over me as he got out of bed, and I breathed in relief.

"Are you hungry?" he asked.

"Not yet," I said, sitting up.

Bare chested, he stood by the bed, watching me with green eyes that were becoming less unsettling. His gaze moved over my face. Now that I'd met another of his kind and had someone for comparison, I realized Drav didn't look at me the same way as Ghua. Ghua watched me with open curiosity, like a visitor at the zoo. Drav studied me with an expression that said I meant something more. The idea made my stomach dip and dance.

"I'm going to use the bathroom. Without an audience," I said, needing to escape his scrutiny.

He didn't try to follow me when I left the room. I closed myself in the bathroom and looked in the mirror. My cheeks were flushed and my stomach was still twisting and dipping at the way he'd held me. Why had Drav taken an interest in me? Every person he'd encountered since we'd met, he'd killed. He said he hadn't killed me because I was a girl, but what about all the infected females? He'd never hesitated to behead them.

I splashed water on my face to settle my confused thoughts. It didn't really help much. After using the toilet and washing my hands, I hesitated to leave. Had I been smart enough to grab my bag when I'd left the room, I could have brushed my teeth and taken a few more minutes for myself. Instead, I did a quick swish and rinse with water then opened the door.

Drav stood in the hallway. He wore his too small shirt again.

"You might want to look in the closets for something that fits better. That looks weird on you."

He didn't do as I suggested. Instead, he followed me to the kitchen. The window near the sink gave a view of the dusky sky. Another day almost gone. What day was it? Did it even matter? There weren't any schedules to cling to anymore. Just the drive to keep moving. To get to the cabin and ensure my family was safe. The sooner we ate, the sooner we could leave.

I took the eggs out of the fridge and dug some sausage

out of the freezer for a big breakfast. Well, dinner, since the sun was close to setting. While the sausage fried, I grabbed my bag and brushed my teeth. Ghua had taken a seat at the table by the time I returned to the kitchen. Ignoring him and his scrutiny, I scrambled some eggs and grabbed three clean plates.

Neither said anything as I set the food before them. Drav again watched me pick up the fork and waited until I'd taken the first bite before trying his own food, which seemed to annoy Ghua. I couldn't wait to leave him. The company of one shadow man was enough for me.

When I finished eating, I took my plate to the sink, washed it, and filled up the water bottle that I'd kept in my bag.

"We ready to go?" I asked Drav.

He glanced at the now dark window.

"Yes, Mya go outside."

"Good." I moved toward the door and, with disappointment, watched Ghua follow Drav.

Outside the house, Ghua gave Drav a clap on his back and then walked away, heading in the direction of Oklahoma City. Drav motioned for me to start through the trees, continuing our way north.

"Everything came from the south, didn't it?"

"Yes."

"Then why is he going back that way?"

"You talk and I learn."

"What the heck does that mean?"

"No word for why he is going back that way."

"Ah." We really needed to up his vocabulary. Just not while we were walking in the zombie infested dark where hellhounds might also roam.

We traveled in silence for an hour before we came to our next major highway. Most roads came and went, barely discernable in the weak moonlight. This highway differed not because of the divided lanes but because of the distant light. Drav didn't try to stop me as I continued toward the far-off beacon. It wasn't until we'd moved much closer that I saw floodlights illuminated the on and off ramps and the over pass. A generator rattled loudly, somewhere near the center of the bridge, the noise blending with the hum of electricity. Excitement bloomed in my chest. Humans had put this here.

Movement to our left caught Drav's attention. He stepped in front of me and stopped our progress.

Frustrated, I leaned to look around him. Before I could ask what he was doing, an infected came sprinting into the light near the on ramp. Its awkward gait and the loose way its arms swung at its sides gave me the shivers. A gun shot rang out. The infected jerked backwards, as if hit in the head, and fell. On the bridge, a person stood and walked to where it had gone down.

"There's people, Drav," I said.

"Mya, no," he said quietly, turning to look down at me with a scowl.

"You seem to like me well-enough. You might like more people if you just try," I said. It wasn't just my desire to be with my own kind that prodded me forward but the need to see who guarded the bridge on the route my parents and Ryan would have taken to the cabin.

"Mya, no."

"What if we stand by those trees and just watch for a while? Maybe you'll change your mind," I said, hopefully.

His gaze swept over my face.

"We go by the trees," he said, nudging me toward their safety.

Grateful not to hear another "Mya, no," I willingly complied. Once hidden in the shadows of the barren branches, I watched the lit area for signs of the shooter again.

It took a few minutes before I spotted movement. A single figure walked the length of the overpass from the edge of the light to the right to the edge of the light to the left. As I watched something to our right caught my attention. A glint of grey moved against the black, and it made my stomach dip in fear.

"Can you see what's over there?" I asked Drav, pointing.

"A human."

Relief flooded me that it wasn't another shadow man. I didn't want to have to go through the whole boobs and no penis thing again.

"How many humans are out there?"

"No words," he said, and I quickly counted up to twenty.

"Seven humans."

Goosebumps broke out on my skin from my head to my toes. Seven seemed like such a little number. But seven survivors in one place...seven who had set up lights as if they knew it would keep them safer from the hellhounds and from—I glanced at Drav and felt a tinge of guilt that I seemed safe with him while others were not.

However, the number showed me a possibility of surviving without Drav and gave me hope.

"Drav, my parents would have driven this way. I want to ask these people how long they've been here and if they saw a red car with two men and a woman."

"It's not safe."

"Why? They won't shoot me. You stay here. I'll come back when I'm done talking to them." I only managed a step before he blocked my way.

"Stop. Wait."

Drav turned and pointed toward a light coming from the south. A car.

"We got a live one," a man yelled. The phrase echoed what Charles and his group had said when they saw me. It boomed in the dark from somewhere near the bridge. Were these people military, too? Part of the Tinker evacuation?

I looked toward the bridge and saw the man on the overpass move to the center of the lit area. He held his arms up, waving the car to a stop. When the car approached, it slowed.

The man waited until the vehicle stopped then walked to the driver's side. He leaned toward the window and stayed there. It remained hard to see more detail from our distance and impossible to hear anything.

"Can you hear what they're saying?" I asked quietly.

"No."

Disappointed, I watched and waited. After a moment, the person on the bridge straightened and pointed to the north.

Another moment passed before he backed away from the car and the driver's door opened.

"I really wish I could hear what's going on," I said. "The car made it here okay. There doesn't seem to be any hellhounds around. Let's just move closer. I'll be safe in the light when I talk to them."

"Wait," Drav said again, not taking his eyes from the bridge.

"You're really starting to annoy me, Drav." I almost said he couldn't stop me from doing what I wanted, but it'd be a lie. He'd stopped me before, and if he wanted to, he'd keep stopping me.

Frustrated, I crossed my arms and continued to watch the driver get out of the car. As soon as he left the car, another man, this one held a gun, stepped from the shadows to the north.

"Is he pointing the gun at the driver?"

Drav remained quiet as we watched the original person on the bridge step forward and open the back door. Several times he went to the back and took a few steps away, as if unloading something. The enraged driver stepped forward and talked with his arms. His voice rose, and I caught some of what he was saying.

"Bullshit...supplies for everyone...it'll come..."

Several scenarios ran through my head but the one that made the most sense was that the men on the bridge were military and collecting supplies for the evacuated survivors. But if that was the case, why take from a single person? There were plenty of supplies in the city from what I'd seen. That is, if they were brave enough to face the infected to get the supplies.

Maybe the person in the car had come from the survivor camp. Maybe he was delivering supplies to these guys? I mean, they had light and a generator, but with no houses nearby they had no convenient food source. Of course they would need supplies, too. But he said supplies for everyone. I wasn't sure what to think.

As soon as the back door closed, the driver got into the car and squealed north, blaring his horn. The man with the gun pointed the rifle at the vehicle. Fear seemed to solidify into a heavy ball in my stomach. Who were these men? The original man called out for him to lower his weapon.

"He just brought the infected to us," the man with the gun called.

"All the more reason to save the bullets. Back to your post."

His words reassured me slightly. Still, I second-guessed my need to approach them. I would find out if my family went this way when I got to the cabin. But, what would we do next? How long would my family and I be safe at the cabin? Charles mentioned a safe zone but not its location. I needed to know where.

"We go, Mya," Drav said.

"No. I think they're with the military. They can tell us where the survivors are, so when I find my family, we'll know where it's safe for us to go."

Drav turned to look at me. Something in his gaze made me feel really guilty for saying what I had. Did he really think

I'd want to stay with him after I reached my family?

"Drav, I—"

A branch snapped behind me. Drav's head jerked toward the sound.

Sixteen

"I know you're out there," a voice said softly. "I heard you talking."

Drav's lips pulled back to show his teeth.

"Drav," I whispered, reaching out to grab his hand. "Please don't kill him. Please let me talk to him. Then we can go."

He looked down at me.

"Not safe."

"It will be. I promise."

He grunted and then vanished.

"I'm over here," I said, nervously. I worried Drav would change his mind.

A rustle of movement came from further within the trees. A moment later, a man dressed in dark clothes stepped out. He carried some kind of rifle loosely in the crook of his arm and looked me over carefully before speaking.

"Where'd you come from?"

"Oklahoma City. I'm looking for my family. How long have you guys been watching the bridge? They would have passed through this way the night the hellhounds attacked."

He made an odd sound between a laugh and a snort.

"Hellhounds. That about sums them up. And they strike

every night, sweetheart. How'd you manage to get this far?"

"I avoid the roads," I said, not knowing what other excuse he'd buy. I certainly wasn't going to admit Drav had helped me. Based on what Charles had said and all the killing that Drav had done, this guy wouldn't have believed me.

"Who were you talking to?"

"Myself. I know noise attracts those things, but sometimes the quiet's worse, you know?"

He didn't say anything. His eyes just slowly traveled the length of me once more, then he tilted his head, considering me.

"They would have been in a red car. Two men and a woman." He still didn't say anything. His silence and Drav's warning were making me nervous.

"Never mind. I'll just keep going."

"Can you pay the price?" he asked, finally.

"What are you talking about?"

"Supplies for passage, little lady. But, in your case, information. Although, I might be willing to trade for something else."

My heart leapt to my throat as I realized I'd misunderstood everything.

"You're not with Tinker."

A harsh smile twisted his lips.

"Fuck no. Like we wanted to be herded into some over-crowded fence like a bunch of animals. We'll take our chances out here. There are plenty of opportunities out in the woods. I mean, look at you."

His eyes slid over me in a skin-crawling way.

Drav had been right. It wasn't safe. I should have believed him.

"I'm okay without the information," I said, starting to back up. "I'll just—"

I stepped wrong, twisting my ankle, and crying out as I fell.

"Shut up," the man said as I landed hard on my ass.

Wincing at the pain in my tailbone, I looked up at the man. He stood over me, his rifle turned so the butt end was aimed at my head.

"How are you still alive?" He drew the rifle back. My heart jumped to my throat.

Behind him, a familiar shadow moved. Drav's eyes glittered with anger as he stalked forward. Relief calmed me enough to have a measure of concern for the asshole with the gun as Drav reached us. My fellow human obviously wasn't nice, but did that mean he should die for it?

"No head ripping," I said.

Drav fisted one hand and raised it high. Unaware, the man looked at me with angry confusion.

"What the hell are you—"

Drav brought his fist down, hitting the man squarely on the top of his head. The man fell forward, almost landing on top of me. I stared at the fallen body for a second. The leaves by his mouth moved slightly. He was knocked out but still alive. Good.

Drav squatted down beside me. Tearing my gaze from the fallen man, I looked up at Drav. He still looked angry enough to rip off someone's head.

"I'm sorry I didn't listen," I said with sincerity.

The tension in his expression melted away, and he exhaled heavily before cupping the back of my head and touching his forehead against mine.

"You are safe with me."

And I realized that I really was. Safe. Safer with him than my own kind, it seemed. I gently touched his upper arm and leaned against him. His fingers twitched slightly in my hair.

"We go," he said.

Was it my imagination or did it sound like those two words were filled with regret?

He pulled away and offered me his hand. In a hurry to leave the man before he woke, I clasped it and stood. My ankle ached, and I took a minute to brush the dirt and leaves from my pants to give it time to settle down. But it didn't. With each step, my ankle hurt worse.

"Drav," I said, stopping. "I think I did something to my ankle. It hurts to walk."

He glanced down then made the familiar move to hoist me over his shoulder.

"Wait, wait, wait," I said, holding out my hands. "I appreciate the gesture, but it doesn't feel so good when you carry me like that."

He considered me a moment then removed my bag and put it over his shoulder.

"Thanks. Losing the extra weight might help—"

Before I could finish that thought, Drav scooped me up into his arms. He didn't move right away, but stared down at me, as if waiting for my opinion on the new arrangement.

"Ah, this works, I guess." I tentatively wrapped my arm around his shoulder.

He breathed deeply, briefly set his forehead against mine again—I was beginning to think the gesture some kind of hug or something—and then took off running. His speed amazed me. The scenery blurred, and the wind made my eyes tear. I turned my head into his shoulder, which made it difficult to give directions. Drav had to slow every so often so I could lift my head long enough to see where we were. He didn't seem inconvenienced by the interruptions or carrying me. In fact, given the way his fingers occasionally brushed my side, I'd say he rather liked the arrangement.

Although being carried helped my ankle, the backs of my knees soon became sore from the press of his forearm. I tried to ignore it until my calf started to cramp.

"Drav, we need to stop," I said against his shirt. "I'm getting a cramp."

He slowed near a group of trees, not far from the next road we needed to cross, and eased me to my feet. A dull ache throbbed in my ankle, but there were no shooting pains once I put my weight on it. Taking care, I stretched one leg then the other, determined not to let my discomfort slow our progress more than necessary.

Drav watched me closely, his gaze tracking each move I made. His scrutiny didn't bother me as much as it probably should have, and I couldn't help but wonder what would happen after I found my parents.

"I'm fine now. Could I have the bag?" I asked, thirstily.

He shrugged it off his shoulders and handed it to me. I sat

with the bag in my lap and dug out the water bottle. When I looked up, his attention was no longer on me but on the woods to our right. I followed his gaze and saw the dark shape of a house through the trees.

"Stay," he said softly before disappearing into the thicket without further explanation.

The night immediately became more menacing without his presence. I listened for any whisper of noise, my need for a drink no longer important. The breeze rattled some branches, and I jumped at the sound. I wanted to call out to Drav, but not knowing why he'd left, I didn't think it safe to make any noise.

Something rattled to my right where there were no trees. A sick feeling settled in my stomach. Swallowing hard, I slowly turned my head and scanned the shadowy grasses. A shape moved, low to the ground, not far from me, and the rattle reached my ears again. Metallic. I squinted and watched the shape creep closer on four legs. Eyes reflected at me in the weak moonlight. Panic seized my lungs, robbing me of the air I needed to yell for Drav. I opened my mouth anyway. No sound emerged. At least not from me.

A low whine preceded a loud rattle as the thing launched itself at me. I barely had time to register what was happening. One minute I was facing certain death and the next I lay on my back, getting my face bathed by the happiest yellow lab on the planet.

I turned my head and wrapped my arms around its neck in relieved gratitude.

"What a good dog," I crooned, running my hands over its

fur while it continued to attack me with affection.

Suddenly, it moved back and began growling. I sat up and saw Drav stood over us, his expression fierce. He growled in return and stepped toward the dog.

"It wasn't hurting me," I said quickly. "It's a dog. A pet. It's friendly." However, the dog looked anything but friendly with its lips pulled back in a silent snarl.

I put my bottle aside and got to my knees.

"Hey," I said softly. "It's okay. Drav's nice." I patted my leg and the dog moved closer, pressing against me. I pet its head, trying to sooth it, but it continued to growl at Drav.

"Mya. We go. Infected."

My heart dropped. I quickly grabbed the dog's collar, removed it, and tossed it aside. With one last pat for the dog, I stood.

"I'm sorry," I said softly. The infected wouldn't hear the dog now when it ran, but if it stayed...I swallowed and went to Drav.

The dog whined when Drav scooped me up in his arms. Branches broke to our left, and Drav took off running. I looked back at the dog. It growled once at the person emerging from the trees then took off after us. More figures appeared behind the first.

The dog tried to keep up but eventually fell behind, though it still remained well ahead of the infected. I laid my head against Drav's shoulder and tried not to think of that poor dog's desperation. What was happening in the world? Where were all the animals? What would tomorrow bring?

A few times, I felt Drav switch directions only to correct

his course a few minutes later. I didn't raise my head to find out why.

His pace remained consistent through the remainder of the night. The sky gradually brightened with rosy hues and streaks of orange so I could see. The area looked familiar, and the ache in my chest tightened with the fear and anticipation that grew the closer we drew to the cabin.

The sun crested the horizon when we emerged from the trees into the back yard of our family retreat. Sunlight streamed between the naked branches and illuminated the rear of the small cabin. Despite the bright rays, the still air had a bitter chill to it.

"You can put me down."

Drav squinted against the light as he glowered at the back of the quaint little building. I wiggled but his hold on me tightened.

"Seriously, Drav. Put me down. I'm sore from being carried like this, too." He relented and set me on my feet.

"Stay here." I took one step toward the back door, eager to get into the house.

Drav moved in front of me, halting my progress. His lips were a thin line in his displeasure.

"Mya, no. Infected," he said.

"It's okay. My family is in there."

I stepped around him, and he set his hand on my shoulder to stop me. Batting his hand away, I spun to face him with a scowl. After being separated from my family and worrying about their safety for so long, I didn't want to play nice anymore.

"I get that you're worried about infected, but I'm not letting you go first. Think about it, Drav. You and your hounds show up—"

"Not my hounds."

"—and the whole world goes to shit. They're afraid. I'm afraid. Infected people are everywhere, your kind goes around ripping off heads, and nothing feels safe anymore. I won't let you scare my family more by walking into the house first."

Drav grunted, which I took as his agreement. He stayed only a couple of steps behind me when I started forward, but it was better than him taking the lead.

Tension coiled in my stomach as I clasped the doorknob. I took a steadying breath and opened the back door. It led into the laundry room, which led to the kitchen. Inside, everything was dark and quiet. Too quiet.

I stepped into the room and turned on the first light before moving forward. Fear and anticipation had me opening my mouth.

"Mom! Dad! Ryan!" My hopeful calls echoed through the house.

Drav stepped in front of me, a growl deep in his chest. I held still behind him, listening. Nothing moved, and no one answered. A lead weight settled in my stomach.

No. They had to be here. They were.

I stepped around him and moved into the kitchen. Even with the sun streaking through the windows, I flipped the switch on. The kitchen looked neat. Unused. My knees went weak. They hadn't made it. Stumbling forward, I called down the hall.

In the answering silence, my sweeping glance caught on the white piece of paper stuck to the fridge. A small sound escaped me. Drav, who stood off to the side by the pantry, watched me stumble toward the note.

Carefully, I unclipped the letter from the refrigerator. My hands shook and the paper crinkled as I leaned against the counter for support.

Mya,

If you're reading this, we made it here safely, but the military started evacuating the area just after we arrived. We wanted to stay and wait for you, but they're telling us it's not safe here. The infected from Fairview are moving south and those hounds are still in the area. I hope we find you at the Tinker Base before they fly us out. Please stay safe, sweetie.

All our love

Mom, Dad, and Ryan.

PS Hurry up slowpoke.

The last bit appeared to be written in Ryan's messy scrawl. A laugh-snort escaped me. More burst out until I was gasping for air, trying to breathe through my hysteria. I kept missing them. But the cause of my hysteria stemmed from more than that. My entire world no longer existed.

Dreams of finishing college, dating, stupid parties, or watching Ryan graduate high school vanished. I slid down the cabinets. The handle poked me in the shoulder, but I could barely feel it. Infected were everywhere. How could the world possibly come back from this? It couldn't. Humanity was

162

done, and I doubted anyone had any idea how it had happened.

Quaking laughter turned into wracking sobs as I spiraled out of control. I'd only made it this far because of pure, dumb luck. Because of my boobs. The thought sparked another bout of hysterical laughter.

Warm, strong hands lifted me. Arms cradled me. Drav's forehead pressed against mine before I turned my head and wrapped my arms around his neck. He held me while my tears soaked his shirt.

The gentle strokes of his fingers over my head slowly soothed me. Sobs turned to hitched breaths between quieter sniffles. It took a while to realize I sat in his lap, draped against him like a rung-out rag. I was still too shattered to care, though.

We stayed like that as the living room lightened. His stomach growled. Guilt had me lifting my head.

"I'll get us some food," I said without looking at him.

His arms around me didn't loosen.

"No, Mya."

His fingers brushed under my chin, nudging me until I looked up and met his green gaze.

"Mya, shower."

I groaned.

"Drav, I really don't want to do this right now—"

"No. Mya shower. I find food."

Guilt hit me harder. He'd remained quiet the entire time he'd held me, putting aside his need for food to comfort me. I could feel tears threatening again so I quickly hugged him and whispered my thanks before getting off his lap and escaping to the bathroom.

Robotically, I kicked off the shoes I'd forgotten to remove at the door. My reflection distracted me from thoughts of what my mom would have said about shoes in the house.

The tears had made my eyes puffy and red, and a riotous halo of kinked hair sprang from my head, a side effect of Drav removing my braids while he'd held me. I sniffled loudly and cringed at the ache in my head but didn't move to blow my nose. Mud smeared my face. Probably from the dog. No wonder Drav had suggested a shower. I exhaled heavily and opened the bathroom door.

In the room I shared with Ryan, I dug through the drawers until I found a pair of Ryan's old gym shorts and an old t-shirt of mine. I grabbed clean underwear from the dresser and took it all to the bathroom.

While the shower water warmed, I brushed my teeth with the spare toothbrushes Mom had always kept on hand. Thoughts ricocheted around in my mind too quickly to sink in. Nothing seemed real outside the bathroom. I let the world shrink to the current moment and the current goal. Shower. Bathed in the heat of the steam-filled room, I stripped and stepped into the spray. The water soothed my headache as I worked in shampoo then conditioner. The floral scent wrapped around me, a small sliver of normality. It didn't fool me.

I took my time toweling off and lingered after I finished dressing and brushing my hair. The door to the bathroom had stayed shut the entire time, thank goodness. I would need to deal with what had happened and what I would need to do next. But not yet. First, I'd eat. Then, I'd sleep. I couldn't deal with anything more than that. Anything else would have to be put on hold until after.

Drav waited for me in the kitchen. Several cans were open on the table. I didn't have an appetite but sat and picked up my fork. I only managed a few bites before I pushed the rest of the can toward Drav. He didn't try to make me eat more.

As soon as he finished, I stood and went to my bedroom.

Even though heavy clouds filled the sky and muted the light of the sun, I closed the open blinds before laying on my bed. Ryan's bed rested only feet from mine, but Drav didn't even glance at it. He joined me and carefully tucked me close to his side.

I didn't fight the closeness. I needed it too much.

SEVENTEEN

Crack.

I jolted upright in bed, my breathing labored. The room shouldn't have been so dark, even with the blinds closed. It took a moment for the noises around me to register. Rain drummed against the window. I shivered as lightning flashed and cast an eerie blue glow around the room for a split second. Thunder followed, rumbling through the skies and house.

Another bolt lit the room, and Drav's fingers wrapped around my arm with bruising force. The quiet rumble of his growl echoed in my ear. He acted like this was the first storm he had ever experienced. His grip tightened around my waist, tugging me back down to bed. I glanced at the clock on the nightstand behind him. Four in the afternoon. Too early to be up on our new sleep schedule. I rested my head on his shoulder and tried to calm my racing heart.

"It's okay. It's just a storm," I said, for his benefit as much as mine. He didn't move.

"Drav, ease up. You're hurting me." He continued staring out the window, his lips back in a silent snarl.

"Drav!" I set my hand on his cheek and forced his attention back to me.

"It's okay. It's only a storm."

My touch calmed him down a bit. But, there was no way we could travel in this kind of weather. Even with Drav's quickness, I'd probably get sick from the wet and cold.

"The storm will pass, but until it does, we will stay here." He just growled softly. "I think we've slept enough," I added when he didn't loosen his hold. Finally, he let me move.

The chilly air outside of the blankets gave me goosebumps. I nudged the thermostat up and listened to the heat kick in. Drav followed me through the house as I turned on all the lights. It made me feel safer.

Uncertain how to entertain ourselves until the storm blew over, I prowled the cabin for ideas. To keep the focus on family time, my parents had decided to limit the technology here. That meant no TV. I doubted there would be anything airing other than the EAS warning, anyway, but it would have been nice to check. A movie would have been a good way to pass time, too. And, it would have helped Drav learn some new words since we were back to 'Mya, no' a lot while I walked through the house. He didn't like me getting too close to any of the windows or doors while the lightning still streaked across the sky and thunder boomed outside.

In the living room, we had an old buffet filled with various board games. Ryan and I passed a lot of time playing them when we weren't outside. I trailed my hand over the different boxes. Monopoly would last us forever, which wasn't a bad thing, but it might be a bit complicated for someone who was still learning the English language, even if he just needed to hear a word to understand it. Twister brought an unbridled image to mind of Drav's body twisted around me as we tried to maneuver through the game. Nope, absolutely not. However, Yahtzee sat right next to the Twister box.

I removed that box, figuring it would be easy enough. Drav followed me to the living room table and sat beside me as I arranged the game pieces. He picked up one of the dice and inspected it closer. I started explaining the purpose of the dice, cup, score cards, and game.

Two hours later, he was still kicking my ass. For a game of chance, he played annoyingly well.

"Let's take a break," I said.

As I stood, another crack of thunder vibrated the cabin. Fortunately, the storm had calmed down a bit, and Drav's agitation had lessened. I thought the game had helped calm him, too. I, unfortunately, wanted to do something else. Besides, my rumbling stomach had been demanding food for the past fifteen minutes.

We walked down the hall to the kitchen where Drav and I made a simple meal of ramen noodles. Afterward, Drav went straight back to our game, but if I had to hear him yell out Yahtzee one more time, I would need to strangle him.

I looked around the room for something else, and my gaze landed on Mom's old iPod. An idea bloomed in my mind.

"Drav," I said, heading for the little device. "I think you're really going to like this."

I opened the Audible app and scrolled through Mom's book selection until I found one marginally appropriate. A non-fiction book about beekeeping, one of many hobbies Mom always wanted to try. There would be plenty of new words for Drav to learn, and maybe it would keep him busy for a bit.

He watched me closely as I unwound the earbuds and held still as I placed the right one in his ear and the left in mine.

"You'll be able to listen to someone talking and learn new words with this," I said.

As soon as I started the book, he blinked at me and his mouth opened slightly in shock. I grinned.

"Thought you'd like that." I took the earbud from my ear and held it out to him. "You can put this in your other ear so you don't hear the thunder." He took the bud but didn't put it in.

I showed him how to adjust the volume then handed him the device. He was so enthralled he didn't notice me walk away.

Messing with the iPod had reminded me that I should charge my phone. We kept extra chargers at the cabin because it never failed that somebody would forget to pack one. In the bathroom, I dug my phone out of my jeans, which still lay on the floor. The phone turned on but still had no signal. I walked back to the kitchen to get a charger out of the drawer.

After that, I hesitated, unsure what to do next. Sleeping all day and staying awake all night had messed with my internal clock. I wasn't sure if I should be eating, watching TV, or going to class...in my old world. I felt completely lost in the new one. So I wandered through the house, looking at the pictures on the walls, until I got to my parent's room. I sat on their bed and picked up Dad's pillow. A hint of his aftershave drifted to my nose. My eyes watered as I looked around the room and hugged the pillow.

Just before fall semester started, we'd come to the cabin as a family. I'd been working all summer, saving what I could for tuition. Ryan had been working and hanging out with friends, too. Mom had called family time and had insisted on a family retreat. She had packed the coolers. Dad had packed the truck. Those three days had been amazing in so many small ways. The time with my mom, cooking in the kitchen. Canoeing with Dad on the nearby river. Playing volleyball outside.

We weren't the kind of family who didn't like each other. I never recalled a time I'd tried to avoid spending time with my parents or Ryan. Sure, I did stuff with friends, but not for the sole purpose of avoiding family time. Why would I want to? We had fun together. We laughed. We talked. We cared.

I hugged the pillow tighter and swallowed hard. I was afraid. Terrified, really. What if those three days were it? What if I never saw my family again? What if all the good people, like Jack and Charles, were dead and only jackasses like the guys by the bridge were left? Was I really all alone?

No. I wasn't alone. I had Drav. He might not be human or understand much, but he wasn't bad. At least, not with me. And, that was far better than being alone.

I set the pillow back on the bed and went to the living room. Drav hadn't moved from his spot. He looked away from the iPod, which he now held, and watched me cross the room. He still only had one earbud in, probably to listen for me.

"I'm fine," I said. "Thank you. For bringing me here. For keeping me safe. For not ripping my head off like you've done with everyone else."

"I wouldn't do that to you, Mya. Ever."

Wow. A full sentence?

"Uh, thanks. That audio book seems to be helping."

"Yes."

"Well, I'll leave you to it then."

His gaze stayed on me as I went to the cabin's one storage closet.

Mom kept everything from blankets to spare mud boots in the modest space. I dug for ponchos. I'd give the rain until tomorrow night. If it didn't stop by then, we'd be leaving, no matter what.

It proved easy to find something that would fit me, but the largest poncho would be a snug fit for Drav, just like his shirt. That thought had me heading back to my parents' room. The odd clothes, stuff that was new but maybe the wrong size, always found its way to the cabin as spares for guests. When I started going through drawers, I found a big and tall shirt for Drav but also a small photo album. I opened it up and thumbed through pictures of Ryan and me playing in the yard at home and here. We were laughing or smiling in each image. Happy instigators. I missed Ryan. I missed them all so much.

I removed one picture of all of us and tucked the folded memory into my bra before I replaced the album. Carrying everything back to the living room, I set the ponchos on a chair.

"If it's still raining tomorrow, we can wear these," I said, gaining Drav's attention. "And this shirt will fit you better than the one you have on." I tossed the shirt to him, and he caught it in his free hand.

"I'm going to check the freezer and see if there's anything we can make for dinner."

Nothing waited in the freezer but ice cube trays, which unsurprisingly were empty. The fridge had the normal condiments that lasted well and a box of baking soda. With a sigh, I went to the cupboards and found a shake bottle of pancake mix. It was better than another can of fruit.

I had a stack of pancakes ready to eat when I went to check on Drav. He sat in the same spot, still listening to the iPod.

"I made some pancakes if you're hungry."

He didn't seem to hear me. I mentally shrugged, went to the game cabinet, and grabbed a deck of cards.

In the kitchen, I played solitaire while I ate pancakes and applesauce. I grew bored with the cards after a while and busied myself with cleaning up. Standing by the sink, I took my time washing the dishes.

Outside, the rain continued to lash at the windows. Dim outlines of the trees swayed in the wind. If Dad were here, he would probably put on his poncho and his mud boots and go out to check the gas in the generator just in case the storm knocked out the power. He would come in, soaking wet, and Mom would be waiting with a towel at the door. I smiled slightly at the mental image and rinsed my plate.

Lightning flashed, and something moved outside the window. The shape looked heart-stoppingly familiar. I covered my mouth with my hand and watched our neighbor, Doug, shamble along the tree line. When the thunder cracked loudly, he sprinted for several yards then went back to a shamble.

Dad's note about the military evacuating them meant we couldn't stay here long. Going out in the rain might serve as a layer of protection even if I wouldn't be able to see or hear as well. It seemed that Doug couldn't hear well, either.

I finished up with the dishes. The leftover pancakes and applesauce I wrapped up and put in the fridge. The lights flickered when I went back into the living room. Drav watched me cross the room to look out the window. Doug had circled the house.

"There's an infected out there," I said. "Do you think he'll try to get in?"

When I glanced back, Drav no longer sat in his spot. The iPod lay on the cushion, though. I looked out the window. Doug had stopped shambling and faced the side of the house. A moment later, Drav appeared from around the corner. Doug started running toward him. Drav caught him up by the head.

I turned away from the window before I witnessed another beheading, and distracted myself by going to get Drav a towel. However, as soon as he stepped inside, he shook himself like a dog before I could hand it to him.

"Um, this is to dry off if you want it," I said, holding the towel out to him.

"Thank you," he said, taking it.

"Good thing you left the iPod inside. They don't work well when they get wet. Do you want me to back up the book and show you how to pause it? Just in case you need to leave again?"

"No," he said quickly. "I understand."

"Oh. Okay. Good."

He moved past me, tugged off his wet shirt, then picked up the iPod to set the towel on the chair. Without a glance my way, he sat and had the ear bud back in his ear a moment later.

I could appreciate his draw to the device. Being able to understand what I said could be pretty useful to him. Yet a tiny voice in the back of my mind questioned his eagerness. What if his enthusiasm wasn't just to understand me? Would he use the knowledge of our language to hurt uninfected people? I thought of the incident at the bridge and doubted it. I'd asked him not to kill the man and he hadn't.

Giving him one last glance, I went back to the kitchen and played solitaire until four in the morning. A full day—or night—of idle time left me yawning much sooner than expected. I stood with a stretch and glanced at the window. The rain hadn't yet let up. In the living room, Drav still listened to the iPod. The book must have been longer than I'd thought.

"I think I'm going to go to bed," I said.

He turned his head and looked at me. For a moment, I thought he would say something. Instead, he gave a slow nod before focusing on the iPod again. I didn't know beekeeping could be such an interesting topic.

After seeing our infected neighbor in the yard, I felt a little nervous going to bed by myself, but I didn't want to ask Drav to come with me, either. So, after staring at him for another few seconds, I slowly made my way to the bedroom and left the door open.   I made sure the blinds were still closed.

Fully dressed, I got into bed and curled under the covers. When I woke, rain or shine, we'd keep going.

EIGHTEEN

A shiver shook me from my dreams, and I curled tighter under my covers. It took a moment to realize why I shouldn't be so cold. Drav wasn't with me. My eyes popped open.

I sat up and looked around frantically. Something on the floor beside the bed moved. I looked down and met Drav's gaze as he turned to glance at me. He sat next to the bed, an earbud still in his ear. A relieved breath escaped me. He was fine. Why had I assumed he wouldn't be? Not much out there seemed to match his strength.

I rubbed my forehead.

"Did you get any sleep, or have you been listening to that all night?"

"I've been listening all night."

If I wasn't mistaken, a small smile tugged his mouth. I stared for a moment. It was the first smile I could remember seeing.

"Hopefully, you weren't too bored," I said.

His smile changed slightly.

"I wasn't bored at all."

I glanced over at the clock on the night stand but it flashed twelve, leaving me with no idea of how long I'd slept or what time it might be. The subtle, muted light filtering through the blinds didn't help. I could pull them back to check, but a small part of me feared I would see an infected shambling around outside. Of course, last night I hadn't even had to tell Drav before he'd left to dispose of our old neighbor.

Regardless of the hour, I didn't want to spend more time here than necessary, not without knowing what had happened to my family. The note they'd left ran through my head. *Before they fly us out.* Where would they be taken? So far, I had missed them every step of the way. If I didn't get to Tinker in time, I feared I might lose them altogether.

"It sounds like it stopped raining," I said, looking at Drav, who watched me steadily. "Are you ready to travel or do you need some sleep?"

"I don't need any sleep before we travel."

That was good. But, first, we needed to get some food in us and check the weather.

I climbed out of the bed and went to the window. With Drav still nearby on the floor, I bravely nudged the curtain back. Heavy grey clouds blotted out the sun's midday rays, providing enough light for me to see. Remembering the way Drav's eyes had watered, I tugged the curtain open a little more and glanced back at him. He watched me closely as his pupils adjusted to the slight change in light. However, his eyes didn't water.

"You're watching me closely. What is it that you are trying to figure out?"

Wow. Those books really helped.

"I was seeing if the overcast light affected you the same way the sun did."

"You could have asked."

"Uh, sorry." The full conversation we were having seemed too weird after only days of broken ones.

Drav stood. He had changed his shirt. The new one still looked a bit snug.

"You can probably put that away for a while," I said, motioning to the device in his hands. He made no move to remove the earbud still tucked inside of his ear.

"I have much more to learn and would like to bring it with us. Let's get some breakfast. We can head out when we're finished."

More to learn? He sounded just fine to me. Hopefully he'd be willing to listen to me for a bit because, now that he could talk, I desperately wanted to ask him questions.

Drav followed me into the kitchen where I grabbed another bottle of pancake mix.

"Is it all right if I ask you some questions now?" I asked as I added water and started to shake the container.

His steady gaze held me for several long moments.

"Ask me anything, Mya."

"Where did you come from? Why are you here? Not in this house, but here, on earth, destroying things?"

"I'm from a place called Ernisi. I'm not sure what happened. But something broke the barrier and a hole opened to the surface. The hounds and two of my kind escaped first. We followed to see where they'd gone and found this..." He looked around at the cabin. "and you..." His gaze landed on me again.

I pulled out a pan and started warming some oil.

"Ernisi," I said, testing the name. "That's where you lived?"

"Yes."

"And it's underground?" It had to be if a hole opened from above.

"Yes, it would seem so."

"What do you mean, seem so?" I asked as I poured some batter into the pan.

"It has always just been Ernisi. I never thought there might be something above or below our dark sky."

I turned the pancakes and thought about what he'd said.

"That had to be a shock then, having your roof open up."

"It was."

But it hadn't been the only shock. I thought back to when he'd first seen me.

"I have another question, but I don't want to make things weird by asking."

"Nothing will be weird."

I stacked the first batch of pancakes for breakfast—or whatever meal this was. I set the plate on the table and watched him as I asked my next question.

"Why did it shock you that I'm a girl?" I asked.

"Ernisi has no girls."

"No gir—" I closed my mouth abruptly as several thoughts collided in my mind. He had a penis and testicles. He'd shown me both during our first meeting. What the hell were they for if they didn't have girls? That wasn't a question I wanted to ask.

Instead, I finished making the pancakes and sat down to

eat in silence.

After we were both fed, I started to wash the dishes.

"I'm going to take a quick shower," Drav said.

He set my mom's iPod down and went to the bathroom. As I listened for the water to crank on, I heard a tiny voice. I glanced at the device and saw what had kept him so occupied all night.

Ice Planet Barbarians by Ruby Dixon. The cover was a sultry image of a blue skinned male holding a very human female.

My mouth dropped open, and I slowly reached for the earbud and placed it in my ear.

"I don't know if she's humming or saying another one of her strange human words. I lick her breast to distract her, and she moans. Then she reaches down and grips my cock in her hand and strokes me through the leather of my leggings."

My breath choked in my throat. *Oh shit.*

I immediately stopped the book and gazed down the hallway in shock. He'd gotten into my mom's romance novels. I tugged the earbud out and scrolled through the last books he had listened to. Ruby Dixon. All the covers with bare-chested men. He'd only listened to three percent of the damn bee book.

I coiled the earbuds around the iPod and set it back on the table. Thankfully, Drav still lingered in the shower. My cheeks flamed hot at the thought of the things he'd been learning, and I was twice as glad I hadn't asked anything more about why there were no girls.

Determined to pretend I didn't know anything about what

he'd been listening to, I went to the front closet where Mom liked to store everything. Although my bag had the clothes I needed, I wanted to be prepared for anything and knew Dad kept an extra pocket knife around somewhere, as well as a lighter and first aid kit. I hoped to find both in the clutter.

Leaning deep inside the closet in my search, I heard Drav's footsteps and tried not to cringe.

"Mya?"

"Here, in the closet."

I was pulling down a small tote from the shelf when he crowded behind me. He plucked the tote from my hands, and I turned around ready to thank him. The words died when I saw he wore his pants but no shirt. Why wasn't he wearing his shirt? I thought of the men on the romance covers, mentally cringed, and met his gaze.

"Did you want me to braid your hair before we leave?" He spoke the words with such ease in his deep, gravelly voice

"No, I'm fine." No way would I allow him to touch me after what he'd been reading. "Go ahead and finish getting dressed then we can go. I'm almost done in here."

Drav nodded and walked back down the hall.

I refocused on finding the spare pocket knife and any other supplies we could use. I found my old, sturdy hiking boots. My parents and Ryan had gotten me a new pair for my birthday the year before. I'd left these up here in case I ever forgot to bring my new ones. Given the rain, boots might not be a bad idea. I considered the room left in my bag and decided the shoes I'd worn here would fit.

I closed the door to the bedroom, changed clothes, and

braided my hair. Once I finished and packed my new finds into the bag, I came out to the living room where Drav sat on the couch waiting. He stood when he saw me. He had rebraided his hair to look much like it had the first time we'd crossed paths. Had it only been a week ago?

Glancing around the cabin sadly, I kept reminding myself that it was only a place as I prepared to leave. My family was what I missed, and because of the storm, we were already days behind them. We had to get to Tinker.

"Ready?" I asked, hiking the bag up on my shoulder.

"Yes."

He held out the iPod. Now that I knew what he listened to, I hesitated to take it.

"It's probably low on battery. We should leave it here."

"Is there a charger?"

Seriously? How did he know that?

Reluctantly, I nodded and went to grab the iPod charger along with the one for my phone. I'd already tucked my phone into my back pocket, safe and sound. When I had everything, I checked the lock on the front door then led Drav to the back, the way we had come in. It might only be a place but it still held memories, and I didn't want anyone coming in and destroying anything. My thoughts roamed to the men on the overpass. Though our paths had crossed briefly, I now knew what type of people they were. No doubt there were more like them out there.

After locking the back door, Drav and I started off through the trees at a brisk pace. He didn't seem remotely tired from staying up all day. I looked at the late afternoon sky, trying to find just how low the sun might be behind the thick clouds. The consistent grey didn't give me a clue.

From the corner of my eye, I caught Drav watching me. I glanced toward him, but he immediately focused on our surroundings. I frowned but said nothing. Twice more I caught him watching me only to have him quickly look away. He was weirding me out. Or maybe, my imagination was weirding me out.

The cold, damp smell of late fall tickled my nose, and I tried to pay more attention to where we were going than to Drav. The ground, still wet from all the rain, squished under my feet. Although my boots kept my feet dry, they were heavier than my running shoes, and it wasn't long before my steps started to lag. Drav didn't say anything about the pace. He stayed beside me no matter how slowly I walked. Night descended as we continued south.

Twice, he had me stop while he disappeared to take care of a nearby infected. I used each break to lean against a tree or building where I sipped water from my bottle. Each time he returned, I offered it to him as well.

Despite the breaks, I was getting tired. It was a couple of hours later when my feet went out from under me. I yipped and swung my arm out to grab something as I fell. Drav's hand gripped my flailing arm, steadying me. Before I could thank him, his steely arms slipped behind my back and under my legs, and he lifted me up. With me cradled in his arms, he continued to walk as if he hadn't decided to randomly pick me up.

"Um, Drav? You don't have to carry me."

"I don't want you to strain your ankle."

"My ankle is fine now. Seriously, you don't need to carry me."

"I don't mind."

He might not, but I did.

"I'd rather walk."

"And risk injuring yourself if you slip? Are you no longer in a hurry to find your family?"

I shut my mouth. Stupid iPod.

Drav carried me like that a couple hours longer, going about the same speed I had while walking. I couldn't imagine how tired he must be. A light sprinkling of rain gave me the perfect excuse to ask to be set down.

I pulled out the ponchos I had grabbed from the cabin and gave Drav his. Like I'd thought, it fit him snugly but did the job. I tugged mine over my head then slung the bag across my body again, determined to walk some more. Drav didn't argue.

Where the ground had been squishy before, mud now slicked the surface. He started slipping, too, and our progress slowed to a crawl. The poncho kept me from freezing in the cold rain, although not by much, and Drav caught me each time I slid, preventing me from landing face first or ass deep in the slippery earth.

The rain eventually let up, but we didn't stop to remove the ponchos. We kept walking, one foot in front of another. Sleep tugged at me, but with the sky still dark, I refused to quit before the sun rose.

My arms and legs felt like lead. My blinks became longer until I realized I was taking steps with my eyes closed.

Drav touched my arm gently, and I knew I was busted.

"You need to rest. Come, there is a house nearby."

"No, I'm fine. We gotta keep going."

Drav scooped me into his arms again, putting an end to my resistance.

"No, Mya. We won't make it there before sunrise. We need to stop for the night. There's a house ahead," he said, steering us toward what I couldn't see in the dark night.

Giving into my exhaustion, I relaxed in his arms until he slipped and tightened his hold on me. I clung to him the rest of the way to the old farmhouse.

No lights were on when Drav set me down on the porch, with a stern "Stay here." I watched him break the lock and slip inside. Cold wrapped around me, and I tucked my chilled fingers under my arms, trying to warm them.

When Drav reappeared, his gaze dipped briefly to my poncho-covered chest before he met my gaze.

"Is it safe?" I asked.

"It is. Come." He held out his hand for me to take.

I easily slipped my much smaller one into his grasp and let him lead me into the house. The heat was on, and I shivered at the warmth. Drav closed the door behind us, and we both struggled out of our wet ponchos. He took mine from me and hung it on one of the many hooks near the door. I moved further into the house, turning on lights downstairs as I looked around. Another nice place. This one thankfully empty.

Tiredly, I followed Drav upstairs, where he led me to a room with a queen-sized bed.

"Go ahead and change your clothes. I will go downstairs

to find some food."

I nodded absently, tugged my bag off, and rotated my shoulders to relieve some of the stiffness. Taking out the sleep clothes I had used at the cabin, I quickly changed.

I didn't go downstairs for food but crawled under the covers and fell fast asleep.

NINETEEN

I snuggled closer to the heat behind me and tucked my hand under my cheek. The bed was so comfortable and warm. I never wanted to leave it.

Then reality pressed ever so slightly against my backside, and my eyes popped open. That wasn't...it couldn't be his...

Drav's fingers smoothed over my hair, moving the few strands that had escaped from my braid off my face. His warm breath caressed my neck.

I bolted. One minute I lay in bed, the next I was all flying elbows and legs as I fought my way out from under the covers. I didn't stop until a solid bathroom door separated me and the horny demon who'd been snuggling my backside. A soft growl answered the sound of the lock snapping into place.

"Don't you dare break that door," I said, taking a cautious step backward.

"Then unlock it."

"No way in hell."

A moment of silence passed as I stared at the door with wide eyes, waiting for it to explode inward. But it didn't. Instead, he spoke again.

"Why did you run?"

I frantically looked around the space for a reason that did

not involve the raging boner he just had pressed against my butt.

"I needed to pee, Drav. Why else?"

"Then why aren't you peeing?"

"Because you're listening. Go away."

Something thumped on the other side of the door.

"I think you're hiding from me," he said softly. "And I don't like it."

I watched the door nervously, but nothing happened. This new, more communicative Drav confused me in a whole different way, now.

"What are you going to do?"

"Wait for you to come out."

I closed my eyes and mentally groaned. There was no way I would walk out of the bathroom just so he could nudge me back to the bedroom for more snuggle time. I wasn't stupid. Demon or human, if it had a penis, there was a purpose for it. I'd been safe because Drav hadn't known or understood, it seemed. However, those damn romance novels had spelled out the reason for him.

"Fine. You want the truth? You scared me just now, almost as much as you'd scared me the first time we met." Not really, but I didn't want to admit that, not even to myself.

"How?"

"Remember how grabby you were? Remember all the times I told you to stop because it made me uncomfortable? You were doing it again this morning."

"My hands weren't on your breasts. They were on your hair."

I covered my face.

"I can't talk about this with you."

"Then we won't talk. Just open the door."

"No." What if he was standing out there, naked, waiting to pounce? "Now that you can understand, we need some rules."

"Rules?"

"Yeah. You understand that word, right?"

"Yes."

"Good. Rule one. No more touching me whenever you want." I paused, trying to think of another rule that the first one wouldn't already cover.

"And the next rule?" Drav asked when I remained silent.

"No more iPod."

"Fine. Now, open the door."

I stood there for a moment, hesitating. I couldn't stay in the bathroom forever. My family was in Tinker, and I needed his help to get there. So what if he'd sprung some wood while snuggling. Like he'd pointed out, he hadn't been groping me. Just snuggle-business as usual. Taking a fortifying breath, I reached for the knob and opened the door.

Drav slowly looked up from where he'd had his forehead pressed against the door—the thump I'd heard. His tormented green eyes pinned me with guilt. I looked away from the emotion there and wished I hadn't when I saw the bare expanse of his smooth, darkly-chiseled chest. He'd slept with no shirt again.

Don't look lower. Don't look lower.

I did and to my relief, he wore pants and was no longer in

pounce mode.

"You are the only thing I like about this world," he said.

My gaze flew to his as my stomach gave an odd flip at his words.

"Please don't ever run from me."

He held out his hand, not touching me, but silently asking to be touched. It surprised me how much I wanted to take it.

"What's going to happen when we reach the city again?" I asked, not taking his peace offering. "When we find my family, are you going to let me go?"

He slowly lowered his hand.

"I will."

"Honestly, I'm not sure I believe you."

He studied me for a long moment.

"I will let you go because I know you won't go far. We both know you won't be safe for long without me."

He said what I'd been trying not to think since before we'd reached the cabin. Once I did find my family, I had no idea how we'd survive this new world. Our only hope lay in whatever location the military had secured for the survivors. A location that wouldn't welcome Drav.

"And if I am safe without you? Will you let me go?"

"Yes. I will let you go."

I nodded, trying to ignore the tightness in my chest, and reached for the door.

"Now I really do have to pee. Please don't stand out in the hallway. It's weird."

"All right. I'll be in the kitchen."

I closed the door and took my time washing up. When I

reemerged, the hall was empty. I crept back to the room, changed clothes, then reclaimed the bathroom to brush my teeth and rebraid my hair.

With nothing else to delay me, I went to the kitchen. Drav sat at the table, a can of peaches before him and another can near the chair beside him.

"Will you eat with me?"

I nodded and sat beside him. My mouth was already full of peach when he spoke.

"My life was lonely before I came here, but I didn't know loneliness then because all I knew was my day to day life. I understand now, and I don't want to go back to it. When we find your family and it comes time for me to let you go, I will. Until then, I ask for your company."

I choked on my guilt as I swallowed down the peach.

"If my being near you upsets you, I am sorry. I never stopped to think that while your presence was giving me comfort, mine caused you distress. I never intended for that to happen. I will be more considerate in the future."

Aw, hell.

"Drav, you have been considerate. You've kept me safe. And I am forever grateful for that. I didn't mean for it to sound like I don't enjoy being near you. You're different and, sometimes, a little frightening to me."

The vertical slit of his eyes narrowed slightly, and I realized my fear of him as a shadow man or demon, or whatever his species, had faded. My only fear remained of him as a man.

"You're not scary to me anymore." I reached out across

the table and set my hand on his, where it rested beside his untouched fork.

He turned his hand and wrapped his fingers around mine.

"Thank you, Mya."

I gave his hand a light squeeze then let go and quickly ate my breakfast. After I finished eating, Drav went to the bathroom. I waited for him at the table until he was ready to leave.

Dusk muted the clear sky as we stepped outside. Near the garage, an infected heard the backdoor click and ran toward the house.

Drav growled and stepped in front of me protectively. I smiled slightly and stayed in place as he charged the man and tore off his head. The fact that I no longer flinched at that level of violence worried me. My world seemed so scarily different now. Hellhounds. Infected. Corrupt survivors. And, hopefully, decent survivors, too.

I thought of the men at the bridge and how they clung to their light and weapons for safety. Not me. I walked around at night unarmed and without fear because of Drav.

He turned back to me as the body fell to the ground.

"It's safe now, Mya."

I nodded and stepped forward.

The ground felt less muddy and slippery than the night before, and I walked on my own two feet without trouble. As the moon rose, we made good progress, but not good enough. Miles passed and I still didn't see the major highway we would need to cross. The one that signaled we were halfway home.

Stopping, I looked at Drav, whose questioning gaze met

mine. His talk in the kitchen hadn't been a ploy to win his way back into my good graces. He really did care about me.

"We'll get there faster if you carry me, won't we?" I asked.

"Yes. But I would need to touch you."

Obviously. I was moved that he remembered my earlier concerns.

"That's okay."

I'd barely gotten the words out before he had me in his arms. He held me firmly against his chest and looked down at me. The slit of his pupils widened the longer he stared.

"Am I too heavy?" I asked, just to motivate him to start walking.

"No, Mya. You are perfect in my arms."

The way he said it reminded me how perfect he'd found me in his arms when I'd woken up.

"Maybe this isn't a good idea. Maybe we should find a car, instead."

"A car is too loud."

Then he ran. Without much choice, I tucked my face into his shirt to avoid the brisk wind.

After a little less than an hour, he slowed to a jog. I lifted my head and saw a dome of light shining in the distance.

"The same bridge?" I asked in a whisper.

"It is."

"Can we see if they are still there without going too close?"

"We could, but why risk you like that again?"

His concern warmed me.

"There aren't many of us uninfected left. Even though they are douchecanoes, I want to know they are still uninfected."

He grunted and continued walking. When we were close enough to see the bridge, he hesitated for a minute then continued moving, creating more distance. I didn't speak, just looked over his shoulder and watched the bridge growing smaller.

"There are twelve now," he said when the light disappeared behind some trees. "Three men are in the trees where we'd stood the first time."

I felt torn by the news. I didn't like that more had joined the untrustworthy group, but I was glad I wasn't the last uncontaminated human on earth.

"If it's safe, can you put me down so I can walk a bit and stretch my legs?"

"Of course."

His touch lingered a bit as he put me down, but I pretended not to notice.

We walked in silence, and I watched the horizon for the soft glow of city lights.

"You know what really bugs me?" I asked.

"Touching."

I rolled my eyes.

"No. I want to know why we lost communications but not power. If I could use my phone, it would be easy to know where my family is right now. To know they are still alive."

"Phone?"

I dug in my bag and produced the phone I'd turned off

after recharging it at the cabin to conserve the battery.

"My brother and I used to text a lot. His last message said to watch out for the dogs and to stay safe. If this were working, I could send him a message asking where he is." I tossed the phone back in my bag. "Instead, we have to run all over trying to find them."

"I don't mind. It means more time with you."

I hooked my arm around his and leaned into him just a bit, guilt and pity welling up inside of me.

"I know. And I don't mind more time with you, either. But, I do worry that the longer it takes to find my family, the less likely it will be for me to find them uninfected."

He frowned but didn't say anything.

"I think I'm ready for you to carry me again if that's okay."

"It is. Thank you."

TWENTY

He picked me up once more and started running south. I
didn't turn my face into his shirt this time. I couldn't stop
thinking about what reaching the city would mean for him.

"What will you do after we reach Tinker, and I find my
family?" I asked, looking up at him.

He stared straight ahead, a muscle in his jaw twitching.

"Tell me about your family," he said, instead of answering.

"I love them, and they're fun to be around. My mom is a
hobby jumper. She'll try anything. Sometimes the hobbies
stick. Sometimes she loses interest. There was one summer
we tried noodling—that's where you fish with just your hand.
Ryan was really into it. He loved it. I wasn't as into touching
the fish as he was."

"What hobby do you enjoy?"

I smiled at the memory the question brought up.

"When Ryan turned thirteen, my mom decided we were
both old enough to try Fire Poi. It's kinda like dancing with fire
on strings. It's beautiful to watch and makes you feel so
graceful. That was my favorite. I kept it up until I went to
college."

We were quiet for a few more roads as I remembered the
time before the world went to hell.

"And your father? What did he think of your mother's hobbies?"

"He has stars in his eyes when it comes to her."

"How did his eyes not burn out if he had stars in them? Are stars not balls of gas in the sky?"

"I didn't mean it literally. It's just a saying. It means to him, she couldn't really do any wrong. He loves her exactly how she is."

He remained quiet, and I gave into the lash of the wind and turned my head into his shirt.

It wasn't long before Drav slowed, and I looked up. Spread before us were the sprawling lots signaling the outskirts of the city.

"You can set me down," I said quietly. He seemed more willing to listen this time and set me on my feet.

Together, we started the hide and sprint method of working our way into the city. With each block, the number of infected wandering around increased. Although I wanted to avoid the densely infected areas, the fastest way to Tinker was to cut straight through them. I wasn't willing to lose another day. I'd been too late too many times.

Without speaking, I signaled the destination for the next mad dash to Drav. He shook his head and nodded down the road. I waited, watching the houses. A small group of infected suddenly ran from around the side of a house almost a block down. A chill raced down my spine as they slowed as a group and continued down the street toward us.

Drav laid a hand on my back, the only thing that kept me from freaking out completely.

Why were they moving as a group? They hadn't done that before.

In silence, we crouched in the shadows of a truck as the herd shambled past. We didn't move until they suddenly sprinted across the yard two houses down. When they disappeared, I looked at Drav.

He slowly shook his head. No talking. Got it. Then, he lifted me into his arms.

After that, we began a different game of run and sprint. The infected's hearing had grown more acute in just a few days. Most now moved in herds, about four to six in size. A few shambled individually, which I took as a sign of being newly infected. I spotted a single infected person dressed in military fatigues further away and swallowed past a lump of fear.

Empty houses lined the streets. Sheets no longer hung out the windows but lay on lawns or bundled up on the curbs. A few cars still sat in driveways or on the side of the road, but the sight of cars grew a lot less frequent. That meant there'd been human movement since we'd left. That had to be a good sign. However, the continued presence of the herds dampened my hope.

Oklahoma City was a shell of the city it once was. Dead.

Halfway through the city, the herds of infected we encountered grew larger, making progress more difficult. Even with me in his arms, Drav made no sound as he moved. I gratefully clung to him, letting him navigate through the danger.

We entered a neighborhood that must have been

scheduled for garbage pickup on the day everything went to hell. Bins lay tipped over in driveways and on lawns. Litter cluttered the sides of the road and against the houses.

Drav unexpectedly sprinted toward a car and put me down. Without needing to be told, I squatted beside him and watched the end of the street where he was staring.

A herd of at least twenty infected shuffled into view on a cross road. Men and women. Even a child. They all moved the same...as if coordinated. They turned onto our road, and I tried to control my breathing and remain calm. It proved difficult, though. Only Drav's presence next to me kept me from complete panic as they drew closer with every shuffling step.

The car's trunk obstructed my view of their progress, which was probably for the best. Each scrape of their approach made me flinch. Drav's hand settled on my shoulder.

One of the shamblers kicked a discarded bottle which rolled under the car and stopped by my foot. The shuffling stopped. My gaze locked with Drav's. My eyes widened while my breath remained caught in my throat. I started to reach for him, ready for him to take off with me but the shuffling resumed down the road.

I released a quiet breath and offered Drav a relieved smile. Tension lingered around his eyes as he gave me a tight smile in return. Neither of us moved.

My need to find my family, to make sure they were safe, was putting both of us at risk. I wasn't stupid enough to think I could make it to Tinker without Drav's help. But, I was smart enough to know he wouldn't be able to take me right to the front door.

The other healthy humans at Tinker probably wouldn't take too kindly to a shadow man. Especially if Charles had made it back. A shiver ran down my spine. The last time I saw Charles, he had shot at me. Yeah, in his own morbid way he had been trying to save me because he thought death favorable over being taken by a demon. That mindset just reinforced why I couldn't take Drav with me to Tinker. I didn't want to see him hurt. Yet, as I looked at him, I knew he would resist leaving my side when the time came.

Once the herd of infected disappeared, I jerked my chin toward the fenced in, lit house across the street. After that close call, I needed a few minutes to calm down and let the shaking stop. Drav nodded and picked me up. In seconds, we stood by the back door. The lock had already been broken. Drav eased it open and moved inside. I waited until he came back and motioned for me to enter.

"I need to use the bathroom," I said softly after he closed the door.

He followed me around the corner and stayed in the hall while I shut the door. With all the stealth we'd been using, the sound of me peeing made me cringe, and I hoped the house was well-insulated. I didn't want to be trapped inside, surrounded by a pack of infected.

Not daring to flush, I washed my hands and opened the door.

"Are you hungry?" Drav asked quietly.

"No. I just want to get to Tinker. We don't have much

time until the sun comes up."

I would feel better if he could at least get me to the edge of the compound, but I also didn't want to leave him stranded in the sunlight.

"Hang on a sec."

I went to the kitchen and rummaged through the drawers in the buffet to see if they had any sunglasses stashed there. I found a pair of reflective aviators...a much better fit than the sparkly, glammed up glasses I'd found him the first time in the city. I turned and discovered him right behind me.

"Found you a new pair of sunglasses." I offered them up.

Drav leaned down, and I placed the glasses on his face. My fingertips brushed against his cheeks. I swallowed. My reflection looked back at me. Wayward strands of my hair stuck out at odd ends.

"They look good on you," I said with a smile.

He didn't comment, just held his hand out for me.

Taking Drav's hand, I followed him to the door while an anxious excitement prickled over my skin. It felt strange not holing up somewhere for the approaching day. But we were so close. Even if my new night-time was slowly approaching, the stress and exhaustion that had pulled at me, melted away. Soon I'd be with my parents and Ryan. I wasn't sure I would ever let them out of my sight again.

The moment we stepped outside, Drav released my hand and caught me up in his arms. He looked down at me, his expression subdued, and some of my excitement faded as his words came back to me. He'd said he had been lonely but that he hadn't known it until he'd met me. Yet, he would willingly let me go and return to that loneliness because I'd asked him to. My heart hurt for him.

He leaned toward me. The gentle curve of his lips held my attention. A rush of hot and cold zipped through me the closer he came. The world narrowed to the feel of his warm breath caressing my skin. My heart beat wildly in anticipation, any fear or doubt completely forgotten. At the last moment, he tilted his head and briefly set his forehead on mine. Regret consumed me. Then, I gently cupped his cheek and returned his version of a hug.

He exhaled heavily, lifted his head, then took a running start to jump the fence. He didn't set me on my feet. Safe in his arms, we left the subdivision and made our way through the rest of the city, clearing the last of the houses well before sunrise.

Beside the road that led to Tinker, he stopped and let me walk. The infected out here were scarce, and we reached the golf course near the military base without incident. As we stood in the shadows of the trees, a small, pessimistic part of my brain wondered if we would find the military base under attack by the infected. But that wasn't the case.

Tinker lay quietly before us, the area lit by so many utility lights that Drav squinted behind his sunglasses.

The infected weren't around but neither, it seemed, were the humans.

"It looks empty," I said softly.

"It does."

Empty meant safe for me to go the rest of the way on my own. I studied his profile as he continued to watch the airstrip and the buildings beyond.

"I would have never made it to the cabin or back to here without you," I said, with an aching heart. "Thank you for looking out for me. I hope you find your friends." I hugged him spontaneously. His arms immediately wrapped around me in return. How had a creature so alien and frightening become so comforting?

When I moved to pull back, he was a little slower to release me.

"I don't want to wait anymore, Drav." Dragging out leaving would only make it harder for him. For both of us.

"It's time for me to go."

TWENTY-ONE

"No, Mya. You will not go in there alone." Drav reached up and gently smoothed back some of my escaping hair.

"Drav, humans with guns will shoot at you if you go with me. What if you get shot again?"

"Then I will remove the head from the one who shot me."

Yeah, that's what I figured he'd do.

"You're a giant pain in my butt, you know that?"

He tilted his head, a look of concern pulling at his features, and I rolled my eyes.

"No, you are not literally causing me pain, you're just annoying me." I sighed. "I don't want to see you hurt."

"Then you understand why I can't leave you yet."

I shook my head at him. He was making this hard on both of us.

"Please, Drav."

"I would do anything for you, but not this. I'll leave you when you find your family. Not before."

I knew arguing would be useless and would only draw unwanted attention from humans and infected alike. So, I sighed and threaded my fingers through his.

"Will you at least hang back a little and let me go first?"

"No. We go together."

I glanced at the main gate again. My frustration built. As much as I wanted to see a living human to know that the base wasn't as abandoned as it looked, I really hoped there wouldn't be one popping up as soon as we approached.

"You're so stubborn. Fine. Let's go."

I released his hand, in case he needed to run, and started forward. We walked silently over the dead greens and across the pavement toward the gate. No one stepped from the guard house or from behind the thick lane dividers as we approached. Nothing moved but the light breeze and a piece of paper taped to the window.

I stepped closer to read the rain-smudged ink.

"Proceed to the air strip," I read softly for Drav's benefit.

Looking away from the note, I met his gaze.

"Are you sure you won't stay here?"

"I'm not leaving you, Mya."

I looked beyond the gate. Although I had high school friends who'd joined the Air Force, I'd never been on the base before and wasn't sure where to go. A large, empty parking lot stretched from the road to another building. I started walking toward the structure until I could read the sign. The Commissary. Someone had painted "Cleared of supplies" across the front of the building.

Uncomfortable in the open, I picked up my pace and jogged toward the building then turned right and followed the store fronts. Drav kept up with me as we passed each business. All had the same message painted on their doors and windows as the Commissary, and I knew everything had been cleared and taken to the secured location Charles had mentioned.

However, seeing inside the empty restaurants only fed my fears. The whole place felt too quiet. No men with guns to guard survivors waiting to be flown out. I thought of all the infected roaming the streets, the one I'd spotted dressed in fatigues, and the lack of houses with rescue needed signs, and picked up my pace as I jogged across an expanse of dried grass. We passed another fast food place, tagged with the word "clear," then ran along another road parallel to more stores.

Ahead, I spotted the airstrip.

"Almost there," I panted.

I didn't slow until we reached the edge of the field-like expanse of lawn. To our left, a sea of empty blacktop. To our right, the long airstrip. Straight ahead, a long length of chain-link fence. The dirt mounded around the posts indicated it was a new addition.

The fence didn't protect anything. Its straight line ran less than fifteen feet long and parallel to the air strip. Papers littered the surface of the fence and fluttered in the wind.

With a sinking feeling in my stomach, I went to the fence and looked at the papers. Notes and letters to loved ones left behind. Pictures of people who were missing. All of it left behind by the survivors evacuated from the base.

I pulled out the picture of my family that I had moved to my pocket.

"Help me look for them. Or a picture of me," I said, handing Drav the photo.

He didn't tell me the effort would be a waste of precious time or that the sun was less than an hour from rising. He took the photo, looked at my family, and then started looking at each photo on the fence. I went to the other end and did the same. I didn't just look at the photos but examined the letters too. Minutes passed as I searched and read. So many families ripped apart. So many lost. Some of the notes were goodbyes to family already known to be infected. An ache grew in my chest with each foot of fence I inspected without anything from my family.

"Mya," Drav said, softly.

I looked up as he pulled a photo from a place on the fence before him.

"This is you," he said.

I rushed to his side and stared at the high school picture of me. Four years had changed me a lot. Yet, Drav had recognized the girl with the shoulder-length haircut and heavy makeup job. Hope washed through me, and I looked at the fence. They'd made it here. How long ago? Had they actually gotten on a plane?

"Where did you pull it from?" I asked.

"Here." He pointed to the empty space I'd been staring at. A space surrounded by images of other people. Letters to other families. Nothing from mine.

I swallowed in an attempt to ease the tightness growing in my throat and took the photo from Drav. It was something. At least one of them had been here.

"There is a mark on the back," he said.

I turned the photo over, and my eyes started to water.

We haven't lost hope. We will see you soon.

"We. They're still alive, Drav." I sniffled and wiped at my

eyes and nose before looking at the fence again then the buildings beyond. I needed to know where they'd gone.

"How am I always just behind them?" I said, more to myself than Drav. He seemed to understand because he didn't answer.

I went back to reading the letters on the fence. Near the center, I found one with useful information.

"Drav, look at this," I said with quiet excitement.

"What is it?"

"A notice. The city's been evacuated, but any survivors should wait here. It says they will do a noon fly over and pick up anyone they've missed."

"They want you to wait in the open, without protection?"

"Well, once the sun is up—"

"The infected are not bothered by the sun. It isn't safe."

"What other choice do I have?"

He didn't say anything as he continued to look at me from behind his sunglasses.

"It'll be okay," I said. "I'll be with my family soon. You should go."

He looked away, the muscle in his jaw twitching again.

Before he could say anything, a phone started to ring. Loudly. Another joined it. Then another. I turned a slow circle, hearing ringing coming from everywhere, and realized what it meant.

"Communications are back. Drav, we need to get to the nearest phone," I said.

He picked me up without question but didn't start running.

"I don't like this. The infected will come."

"No, listen. The phones are ringing everywhere, not just here. They won't know where to run."

"They'll know to run toward the noise."

"Please, Drav. Just go!" I pointed toward the large buildings north of us, and he took off running.

It wasn't hard for him to break into the empty hangers. He set me on my feet and closed the door behind us. I ran for the nearest phone, getting it by the seventh ring. I pressed the receiver to my ear, trying to hear something besides my racing heart.

"State of emergency has been declared for Oklahoma City. Uninfected residents have been cleared. Any remaining survivors should clear city limits within the hour." The message just kept repeating after that.

I slowly hung up the phone. Thoughts whirled in my mind as I turned to look at Drav, who watched the door. As if sensing my regard, he glanced at me.

"What was that?" he asked.

"A message. A state of emergency has been declared for the city. It said we need to clear city limits within the hour." But, why clear the city limits? And who declared the emergency? There was no one here.

"This doesn't make sense," I said, looking at the empty hanger. "Why declare a state of emergency now? Everything is already gone? All that's left are infected. And that automatic message probably just pissed off all of them." I frowned, thinking again. "Why are the phones suddenly working now?"

Drav gave a very human looking shrug.

"What do you want to do? Leave or wait for the plane?" he asked.

"I don't know. The infected were acting weird, right? Maybe the call is to warn survivors to leave the suburbs because of that." Yet, that didn't feel right. Again, why call now? Why hadn't an automated call gone through during the hellhound wave to warn people to stay inside? Instead, phone service had just vanished.

The phone started ringing again. I picked it up and listened to the same words before quickly hanging up. Dread settled heavily in my stomach.

"We need to leave," Drav said, echoing what I'd been thinking.

"Agreed." He peered through the window then picked me up.

Outside, he didn't head back toward the airstrip but stuck close to the buildings. His slow, stealthy movements and the constant distant ringing crawled under my skin until tension coiled tightly around my heart and lungs.

"I don't want to leave again," I said. "But, this place feels all wrong and is weirding me out."

Drav slowed to look down at me.

"I think maybe we should leave city limits like the message said. Just for today. We don't need to go far, just somewhere we can keep an eye on things and figure out what's going on."

"Mya, slow your breathing." He leaned his forehead against mine, the cool rims of his glasses biting into my skin.

But I didn't mind. It was real, and it helped me realize I'd been starting to panic.

I closed my eyes and took a deep, slow breath before opening them again. As soon as I did, he pulled back to look at me.

"Better?" he asked.

"A little."

The phones stopped, the sudden silence as unnerving as the collective ringing. Drav turned his head, looking at the open expanse of parking lot and further to the dead grass beyond. His arms tightened around me slightly, which scared me.

As I focused on the area, shadows moved just beyond.

"Infected?" I whispered.

"No. Ghua and others."

A cold sweat broke out over my skin as I counted shape after shape emerging from the far tree line in the predawn light. Six shadow men ran together toward us.

"Drav, I think we should go."

"You are safe with me, Mya."

"From infected and hellhounds, but you let Ghua sniff me."

He grunted but still didn't move.

"At least put me down."

"You will stay?"

He really thought I'd try to outrun six demon men?

"Yes. I'll stay." Like I'd go anywhere alone with all the phones ringing.

Even with my promise to Drav, it was hard not to turn and

run at the sight of six large shadow men sprinting toward us. And they weren't even going their full speed. Ghua's familiar face stuck out from the others.

"Drav!" he said, as he made it to us first.

His sharp, eerie yellow eyes swept over me. His gaze had lost some of its curiosity since I had last seen him but those of his approaching companions worried me. I shivered and moved closer to Drav. He better not let them sniff me.

Drav stepped in front of me and partially blocked me from their view. I reached up and laid my hand on his back, in thanks. However, Drav's gesture proved pointless when the others arrived and crowded around us.

Drav tensed under my touch as one of the shadow men walked around the half circle they had created to get a better look at me. He stood shorter than Drav but seemed more heavily muscled. His skin was even darker than Ghua's, and his eyes were more of a mustard yellow. His gaze swept over me, lingering here and there.

"What are you all doing here?" Drav asked in English.

Ghua said something, drawing my attention back to him and the others. It was unfair they could understand me but I couldn't understand them.

"No," Drav said, turning to look at the man who had stepped around us. Drav's fingers brushed against my hip, and he tugged me to his side.

"What's going on? Why are they here?"

"Ghua told them about you. They have come to see some women for themselves and crossed our trail."

Worry twisted around my heart like a vise. Drav had said

they didn't have women in their world. And although it concerned me that I'd sparked their interest, I still felt a small measure of safety. Not only did I trust Drav, but I also knew Drav hadn't seemed to grasp the point of a girl until the stupid audiobooks, which I refused to think about further.

"Did they find any?"

Ghua spoke briefly before Drav translated.

"The ones with guns took the healthy, leaving only infected females. After they removed the head of one, they looked—"

"Okay. That's enough. I really don't want to hear any more."

Mustard eyes stepped closer, claiming my attention, his focused intensity so like Ghua's the first time we'd met. It worried me. When the new shadow man spoke, I couldn't understand a single thing he said. But the way Drav growled and stepped in front of me let me know it wasn't good.

Twenty-Two

"No," Drav said.

"Drav? What's going on?"

"Phusty wasn't there to see the infected female. He doesn't believe you have no penis and wants to see your breasts and pussy."

I choked, hearing that last word. Drav was never getting that iPod back.

"Yes," the one who I assumed was Phusty said. "Show no penis."

"No, she doesn't want to," Drav said, answering for me. "We are not here to look at women. We are here to search and learn."

Phusty scowled. With a low, angry voice, he spoke to Drav in their language.

"I lost their trail on one of the many roads that crosses this land. I was searching when I found Mya, and I continued searching while learning about this place," Drav answered in English.

I wasn't sure what was going on, but some of my worries about Drav learning our language started to resurface. What had he been searching for?

Phusty snorted, said several more incomprehensible

words, then gestured in Drav's direction.

Drav began to speak in his language, and a pang of hurt stabbed at me along with my doubt. He knew English and knew I wouldn't understand that language, just as I knew they could easily understand mine. Drav was purposely hiding something from me.

Before I could ask what they were talking about, Drav said Ghua's name then mine. Ghua stepped forward in a flash and wrapped his arms around me. Pissed didn't begin to cover how I felt about this betrayal.

"We are not doing this again. Dammit, Drav!"

Since my arms were pinned to my sides because of Ghua's hold, I kicked out with both legs at the man who'd slowly won my trust. Drav, however, missed my awesome display of vengeful fury. The shithead was too busy snarling at Phusty.

"Let me go!"

Ghua's steely grip didn't waver as I kicked and thrashed. It wasn't like before when he'd groped me. This time, his hands stayed clear of my breasts. It didn't matter.

"I swear to God I will bite off your precious man-stick if you don't let me go now, Ghua."

Ghua made a disturbed noise.

"Stay, Mya. Ghua good. Drav friend."

His attempt to communicate penetrated my anger, and I stopped struggling long enough to blow some loose hair out of my face. With a cooler head and a clearer view, I saw why Ghua still held me. Two of the shadow men faced off in the center of their loose circle. Phusty crouched before Drav, his lips peeled back over his canines in a fierce snarl. Drav didn't react but remained tense and ready. What were they doing?

Dread filled me as Phusty lunged toward Drav. Like when Ghua had faced Drav, their movements were almost too fast to track. But, I saw enough to know this was no friendship match like back at the house.

Phusty slammed his fist into Drav's side. The thud made me wince, but it didn't slow Drav. He snaked an arm around Phusty's neck before he could pull back and held him in a chokehold. No one moved to interfere. The only sounds came from the two struggling.

A red hue crept into Phusty's face as Drav exerted a scary amount of force around his neck. The man didn't give up, though. He landed several rapid, brutal blows to Drav's ribs. Drav grunted and stumbled backwards, releasing his hold. Free, Phusty sprang back and crouched low, ready to attack again even while he coughed and sucked in several breaths.

I tapped Ghua's forearm, and he loosened his hold but didn't let go. I didn't mind so much anymore. Gaze fixed on the pair, I watched like the rest of the group.

Phusty stopped coughing, grinned, and said something that caused a low, warning growl to rumble through Drav's chest. Before the sound stopped, Phusty rushed forward again. Drav twisted out of the way at the last second, and Phusty stumbled without a target. As the man flew past, Drav brought his fist down with a meaty thunk onto Phusty's back. The demon spun around quickly and clocked Drav in the face.

The sound of his teeth clacking together had me wincing again, and I almost missed him catch Phusty's arm. Drav gave the appendage a sharp twist, wrenching it behind the other man's back. Phusty's angry gaze met mine, and his lips upturned into a mean smile. In a flash, he flung his head backward, connecting with Drav's face.

I hissed in an empathizing breath and saw Drav's nose start to bleed and his eyes water. The watering could be from the hit to the face or the rising sun.

Phusty tried and failed to pull out of Drav's hold.

"How long are they going to do this?" I asked, Ghua.

"Drav not share Mya. I don't know...talk."

"You don't know the words to tell me?"

"Yes."

I frowned.

Drav drove his knee into the back of the other man's. Phusty buckled, landing hard on his knees before Drav. He yelled something in his language as Drav heaved back on his arm.

One minute I watched Phusty's face contort in pain, the next I was staring at a spatter of blood and gore as Drav pulled Phusty's head clear off.

Bile rose in my throat. I gagged, and Ghua released me. None of the others seemed even mildly upset by what they'd just witnessed. They watched dispassionately as the body fell forward onto the ground. Drav dropped the head near the body, his gaze on me.

My throat felt tight as I tried to wheeze in a breath.

I didn't like Phusty. Hell, from the moment he arrived, he'd freaked me out. Why, then, couldn't I breathe? Why did I feel sick? Why was I shaking? Shock. I'd just watched a fight to the death. It could have been Drav.

Drav moved toward me, covered in Phusty's blood. I reached for him, grabbing his bicep with shaking fingers. His hand cupped the back of my head, and he leaned down and pulled me forward to press his forehead against mine. Blood slicked my skin at the contact. It didn't matter. His comforting green gaze held mine, and slowly the panic began to ebb. He was here. He was alive. I was alive. We were okay. I took one breath then another. My grip on his forearms tightened as I exhaled shakily.

"Mya."

His lips formed my name quietly as if reassuring himself that I was still here. Safe.

"It will be okay. He will not try to claim you again."

"No kidding. You killed him."

"Yes. But, when he awakens he will not try again," he said calmly. He gave my forehead one last press then took a step back, breaking the spell around us.

The others stood near Phusty's body. Ghua nudged it with his foot.

"What are you doing?"

Ghua stopped and looked at me.

"He's dead. Leave him be."

The men around Phusty stopped what they were doing and looked back at me. Drav stepped into their line of view.

"What did you say?"

"He's dead."

Drav's gaze flicked to Phusty then back to me.

"Dead?"

Drav hadn't questioned words before. I didn't understand

why he seemed confused by the word now.

"Drav?"

He didn't say anything. Instead he left me to go to the others, who had been listening to our conversation. They started to speak in their language again. Based on the rise in their voices and their gesturing, they were arguing about something.

Oranges and pinks painted the sky with the rising sun. I shook my head at them and picked up the bag that Drav had dropped at my feet, a reminder of why we were even at the base.

"Do you really have time for this?" I asked, rather loudly.

They didn't seem to hear me. I shouldered the bag and started walking toward the airstrip. I wasn't going to miss another chance to find out if my family was still alive.

"Mya."

I stopped and turned back to see Drav coming toward me. Worry pinched his features. Behind him, the others were picking up Phusty's body and head.

"What's going on?"

"Ghua and the others have decided to take Phusty back," he said, joining me.

I guess it made sense that they would want to bury him or something.

"Okay. You should go with them, Drav."

He reached for my hand and threaded his fingers through mine.

"I'm not leaving you, Mya."

He tugged on my hand lightly and started leading me

toward the airstrip. His words and company warmed me, but I knew he couldn't stay. I waited until we were beside the fence with all the pictures.

"I would never have made it this far without you. Thank you," I said. I rose to my toes and pressed a kiss to his clean cheek then wrapped my arms around his shoulders. He hesitated a moment before hugging me in return. My chest felt tight, and I struggled not to cry. This world was scary because of the shadow men, but it would be scarier without Drav, too.

He held me close until I leaned back.

"Now hurry up, I don't want you having to return home all alone." And that was the truth. I didn't want him to feel lonely again.

"I will wait until the plane arrives."

"Drav, you can't. I won't risk your life because you're stubborn."

"I promised to get you to your family."

He had promised to bring me home. And that had changed along the way. I knew he wanted me safe before he left me. But that meant staying until the plane arrived, something that would put him in too much danger. I couldn't allow that.

"You *have* gotten me to them."

"No. We found your picture, not them. I need to know they are not infected, too, before I leave you."

The note had given me hope they'd made it to safety, uninfected. But I had no way to prove it. That thought set off a tiny explosion in my mind. The phones. With the phones ringing, maybe that meant my cell would work now, too.

"Here. Let me check my phone," I said, quickly digging in my bag. "If I can get a message to them and they answer, will you leave then?"

Drav didn't comment but watched me power on the phone. My heart beat hard in my chest, and my hands shook as I sent a quick message to Ryan's number.

At Tinker base waiting for pickup.

Hope tormented me with a new kind of agony as I stared at the display, waiting.

The sun broke over the horizon, and I looked up at Drav, who squinted painfully. He needed to find shelter now.

I opened my mouth to say so, but the blare of sirens cut me off. Clapping my hands over my ears, I looked up the pole at the nearby speaker that emanated the deafening sound. My eyes widen as I glanced around the empty army base. Why were the sirens going off with no one here?

Drav shoved the bag into my arms, picked me up, and sprinted away from the base and the noise. When he stopped, the alarms still blared in my ears, but the sound was bearable.

"What is that noise?" he asked.

"Sirens. I don't understand why they're going off though. There's no one here but—"

Oh my god.

The phone calls...the evacuation. They wouldn't. Would they?

I lifted the phone that I still clutched and saw Ryan's name. My gaze dropped to the single word he had texted.

Run.

My head snapped up, and I met Drav's unwavering gaze. Above us, something moved in the sky. Several planes. He must have seen the panic and fear in me.

"We need to get out. Now!"

He lifted me in his arms and took off running, heading south. His speed robbed me of air. I looked over his shoulder and watched the base and the city fall behind us.

In the distance, I saw the first bomb fall.

A single word remained burned in my mind.

Run.

The deafening boom and shockwave from the bomb slammed into us, knocking Drav forward. My ears rang, disorienting me further as he stumbled. Heart hammering, I forced myself to look over his shoulder and saw an old tree slowly topple behind us. Beyond it, a giant, misshaped smoke plume rose like a mushroom in the sky. A second bomb erupted not far from that cloud. High over the city, a plane zipped in, and I watched another silent explosion mushroom upward.

My family was still alive and safe somewhere to the north. But a warzone now lay between us, adding to the obstacles I would need to face in order to reach them.

How was I ever going to find them?

Author's Note

Thank you for reading Demon Ember! We hope you enjoyed reading it as much as we enjoyed writing it. Reviews are so important to spread the word about a story you loved or hated. Please consider leaving one and telling a friend about the book.

If you want to keep up to date on our release news, teasers, and special giveaways, please consider subscribing to our newsletters. (We only send periodically, so you won't be overwhelmed.)

Until next time!

Melissa and Becca

Also by **MJ Haag**

Beastly Tales
Depravity
Deceit
Devastation

Lutha Chronicles
Escaping the Lutha
Facing the Lutha

Connect with the author MJHaag.MelissaHaag.com

Also by **Becca Vincenza**

Rebirth Series
Damaged
Healed
Stolen

Merc Series
Freelance
Contracted

Hexed Hearts
Hunters Heart

Connect with the author at BeccaVincenzaAuthor.wordpress.com

Made in the USA
San Bernardino, CA
19 August 2017